AF582773

SMUGGLERS

Moon Crescent Beach
Re-Knew
Spruce Haven
Gray Island
N
Bear Cub Island
Three Hills Island
The Home Coast

SMUGGLERS

Steve Wedlock

and

Steve Dean

Copyright © 2023 by Steve Wedlock and Steve Dean

All rights reserved. In accordance with the US Copyright Act of 1976, the scanning, uploading, and electronic sharing of any part of this book without the permission of the publisher constitutes unlawful piracy and theft of the author's intellectual property. If you would like to use material from the book (other than for review purposes), prior written permission must be obtained by contacting the publisher. Thank you for your support of the author's rights.

Text: Steve Wedlock and Steve Dean
Editor: Gail Kathryn Swift
Cover and Interior Illustrations: Raphael Quek
Cover and Interior Design & Layout: Danielle Smith-Boldt

ISBN 978-1-7379854-3-3 (Paperback)
ISBN 978-1-7379854-6-4 (eBook)

TABLE OF CONTENTS

I must go down to the sea again,
The lonely sea and sky,
I left my shoes and socks down there,
I wonder if they're dry?
—Spike Milligan

PROLOGUE

ABOVE BOARD

Current usage:
In clear view, open, honorable.

Original use:
On the deck, visible, not in the cargo hold.

Two men were lounging on a small beach beside an old shipwreck. The island was some way out from the coast of Maine, uninhabited and rarely visited, perfect for their needs. As usual, the pair were drinking beer and solving the world's problems one at a time. There were several empty bottles on the beach and a few floating in the water, which is why they didn't hear the plane flying towards the island until it was practically above them. The small seaplane was white and had no markings. It flew over the island, circled around it and came back to land just off shore. The door opened, a package was dumped out and the plane moved away, the whole thing taking only a few seconds.

The two men climbed unsteadily to their feet and headed over to the rigid inflatable boat (RIB) pulled up on the shore. By the time the RIB was launched and headed out to sea, the plane was a speck on the horizon, the hum of its engine a fading memory. One man steered the boat while the other, armed with an oar, wrangled the package until he was able to pull it aboard. It was the size of a small suitcase, wrapped in several layers of plastic. Once it was safely aboard, the two men returned to shore and dragged the old RIB onto the beach, leaving the package on it.

One of the men then walked over to the shipwreck and went inside what was left of the wheelhouse. It was an old wooden ship, the timbers still strong even after several months of being exposed to the Atlantic storms that had delivered her here. With a multi-tool, the man fixed an item they'd brought with them to the wall and ran a thin wire across the doorway. He steadied himself on the door frame and slowly stepped over the wire and back onto the beach.

He grinned widely at the other man. "OK, one package collected, surprise package delivered, time to go!"

"Whoever comes snooping around is going to get a lesson they'll never forget."

The two men were getting back into the RIB when they heard the sound of another boat approaching. It was far too late to escape, so they put smiles on their faces and tried to look innocent.

A red speedboat with twin engines pulled up next to them, expertly stopping with a blip of reverse throttle. The man aboard shouted at the pair "What are you still doing here? You should have left a long time ago. Get moving!" The man pulled away to let the RIB head out into open sea and watched them for several minutes to make sure they left, then powered up and headed off at top speed, leaving the RIB bouncing in its wake.

"Who does he think he is, giving us orders?"

"Yeah, too many bosses around here, if you ask me."

"Well, at least we'll be getting a bigger payout if this new plan old Kneasley is working on pans out."

"Yeah, big if."

CHAPTER ONE

AN EARLY START

FITS THE BILL

Current usage:
What is needed or appropriate for the situation.

Original use:
An item as stated in the bill of lading.
(A list of items aboard or being loaded onto the ship.)

Conner Allen guided the small boat across an almost flat calm sea on the first day of their summer break. He was 17 years old now, 5 feet 9 tall, with great gray eyes and short black hair, wearing a plain black T-shirt, faded blue jeans, black sneakers with green laces and an orange compact life jacket. The electric motor pushed them almost silently through the water as they surveyed the area, looking for a potential spot for a marine reserve. "Somewhere around here, I was thinking. Not much sea traffic because there's nowhere for anyone to go apart from to the islands."

Ryan McNeal was sitting on the thwart just in front of Conner and on the starboard side, scanning the area with his bright orange binoculars. He was also 17 but taller than Conner at about 5 feet 10. His eyes were also gray and he'd grown his light brown hair down to his shoulders. He was wearing a dark red T-shirt with a cyborg shark on it, black jeans and black and white sneakers. His life jacket was exactly the same as Conner's. "Certainly no one here now, although it's not quite high season yet."

Dawn, Ryan's sister, was on the port side of the same thwart, studying some notes on her phone. She was 16 now and 5 feet 4 inches tall. She also had gray eyes like her brother, but her hair was blonde and shorter. She was wearing a yellow T-shirt, faded jeans, yellow sneakers and a matching bright yellow life jacket. "Ok, I'm taking down the co-ordinates. That's Crow Head Island ahead, last stop before open ocean."

Terry Shay was sitting on the front thwart directly in front of Dawn. He turned around and asked, "is that head as in headland or is the island shaped like a crow's head?" He was of the Penobscot tribe of Native Americans, also 17 years old, 5 feet 8 tall with black shoulder-length hair, brown eyes and olive-brown skin. As always, he was dressed entirely in green: sneakers, jeans, and T-shirt. While the others used backpacks, he preferred a multi-pocketed jacket, also green, which was stored under the thwart. He'd settled for a lime green life jacket because the added function of such a device was to be seen in the water and dark green wouldn't work. He and Dawn had been dating since last summer. Terry lived a few miles inland with his parents during the winter, so they'd been apart for several weeks.

Dawn smiled. "Must be headland, because it's shaped like a long oval."

"That island would make a good eastern edge to the reserve; it acts as a good break between here and the open sea." Jenna Cushman was almost 18 and the oldest of the group. She was of average build and stood 5 feet 7 tall, with dark brown eyes and short, light brown hair. Of them all, she was the one who's clothing varied the most. Today, she was wearing a red life vest with a light shirt over the top, loose grey shorts and red sneakers. She'd matched her life jacket to her sneakers; she owned at least three combinations in different colors. She was sitting in front of Ryan, on the starboard side of the forward thwart.

It could be said there was a sixth member of the crew; the boat itself. The 18-foot white fiberglass boat had been lovingly restored over the last few years, and converted to run on electricity, mainly by Ryan, with help from Dawn and Conner. It was officially registered as the 'Peggy Sue' but wear and tear had erased the 'P' and the last 'E' and it was now affectionately known as the 'eggy Su'. This was the only part of the boat not restored as the teens had come to like the new "name". The boat had been with them since the start of their adventures, had been sabotaged at one point and nearly sunk, but had remained a constant in their changing lives. Since the conversion, the boat's speed and stealth had proved useful many times over. The boat had previously belonged to a relative of Ryan and Dawn's who had gone backpacking in South America and the teens had been left in charge of the boat. They'd recently heard from the relative and been told they wouldn't be coming back except to visit; so the boat was now officially their property.

Conner, Ryan and Dawn lived permanently in Stonehaven, going to school here and spending most of their spare time together. Conner lived with his parents and younger sister in a house on the edge of town farthest from the sea. Ryan and Dawn lived in the house opposite on the same quiet residential street, with their dad, step-mom and older sister. Conner's parents owned and ran a pizzeria, where Conner sometimes worked to help out. Ryan and Dawn's parents were realtors with their own business and were always busy.

Terry lived inland with his parents for most of the year, moving to their family-owned house on the coast for the summer with his parents, who were both artists. Jenna lived with her three sisters in their dad's huge apartment in DC for most of the year. In the summer they all moved in with their mother and gran in a tiny house in Stonehaven. Like her sisters, she sometimes found it unbearably cramped when they were all home, so she was glad to spend as much time away as she could.

When they were apart, and indeed when they were in the same town, the five of them were in constant contact texting, facetiming or other apps they would discover and test, and they loved to played games together online. Terry was the keenest gamer, owning a PC he'd built himself and a games console, and usually had a couple of games on his phone.

Terry and Jenna were on lookout duty today, in what was considered their usual spots in the boat. The teens rotated seats occasionally and they all took turns at the motor. Most of the time, they all sat where they were sitting now. Terry, who the others said had eyes like an elf, shaded his eyes and looked towards Crow Head Island. "What was that? I saw a flash of metal near the island."

Ryan turned towards the east and scanned around with the binoculars. "Where exactly?"

"On the sea near the southern end of the island."

"Yes, got it." Ryan was silent for a few moments, a small grin appearing on his face. "Well, well, looks like our adventure is starting early this year."

"What is it?" Conner asked.

"A red speedboat. Heading south, going very fast."

"Same as the one that followed us last summer?"

"Sure looks like it!"

Jenna laughed. "Aren't you jumping to conclusions a bit?"

"I don't think I am. Every year something has come up. We had that whole illegal pollution thing, then the sabotaging of the renewable energy equipment, and last year the whole kelp farm? environmental disaster we stopped. So, no." Ryan said all this without lowering his binoculars.

"I'm going to take a bit more convincing," Jenna said.

"Me too," Terry said.

"Yeah, and me, sorry bro."

"I'm with Ryan, let's go check it out." Conner twisted the throttle and raced towards the island.

"We'll never catch him, Con, not even in this," Ryan laughed. "He's too far ahead."

"Maybe it's time for another upgrade."

"Yeah, good idea."

"Didn't you just finish one?" Dawn asked.

"Yes," Ryan grinned, "we upgraded the battery and the motor and tweaked the speed controller. The whole motor assembly is actually lighter and faster, but the battery only lasts about seven percent longer."

"Doesn't feel any faster," Dawn said, her attention mostly on her phone screen. They had no signal out here, but they had charts of the local area stored on each phone and she liked to take notes with it.

Conner shared a look with Ryan, both of them grinning widely, then twisted the throttle all the way open and the 'eggy Su' noticeably increased speed. They had no instruments to show them how fast they were actually going, they simply relied on a timed run between locations to judge their average speed while they were testing their improvements. Despite this, both Ryan and Conner claimed they could tell the boat was faster by the wind and sea spray in their faces.

They soon arrived at Crow Head Island, and Conner steered the boat towards the southern end, keeping a good way from shore but close enough to see if anything was there. Sea traffic was light at the moment in this area, which wasn't on the usual tourist list of things to see in Maine. Ryan scanned the location around where he'd spotted the speedboat and found the remnants of its foamy wake. It was fading now but was still visible as a straight line of white on the blue sea, starting near a long but narrow beach of coarse sand. At the southern end was a wrecked ship, while at the northern end were large boulders that melted into the bedrock.

"Looks like whoever was there was near that old shipwreck. I can't see anyone else. Terry?"

"Nothing. There are markings on the beach, looks like a boat was dragged ashore recently."

After marking the position, Conner took them north and circumnavigated the whole island to check for other people and possible dangers. They'd found nothing else of interest by the time they'd returned to the first beach.

"Ok, I'm taking us in, keep a look out." Conner turned the bow towards the shore, dropping the speed to a fast-walking pace.

As they got closer, they could see the scrape marks and lots of footprints near and around the wreck. There didn't seem to be anyone else around, and aside from the wreck there was nowhere to hide. The uninhabited island was owned by the state of Maine so was considered open to the public, although only those with suitable transport could get here. Locals and tourists alike very rarely stopped by in their boats, but the lack of facilities soon drove them away. Apart from some sea birds, there wasn't much wildlife to see either. The most proliferous inhabitant was a tough, low-growing bush with dark green leaves and small yellow flowers, which covered most of the island.

Conner slowed to a crawl and allowed momentum and the waves to carry the boat forward until it bottomed out on the sand. With practiced ease, Jenna and Terry jumped out with mooring lines and held the boat steady while the others followed. The 'eggy Su' was too heavy to drag onto the beach, so they set the anchor and went off to explore. Terry went first as he had some tracking skills learned from his parents and other tribe members.

"There was a boat here, probably a RIB. Two people, although their footprints are blurry. And look, beer bottles left everywhere. That could be a clue, we know two people who like to relax with a few drinks."

"Marty Whitford and that Nic guy." Ryan nodded.

"Dominic Pelletier," Dawn supplied.

"Lots of people drink beer, lots of people drop litter," Jenna pointed to the usual collection of plastic bottles and scraps of fishing nets scattered along the high-water mark.

"I'm not saying it is them, I'm saying the evidence doesn't prove it's not," Ryan answered.

Terry headed towards the shipwreck, following a single set of footprints right up to it. "I'll just check inside what's left of it."

The wooden vessel had been left above the high-water mark by a recent storm. It was an old fishing boat, about forty-five feet long, with a large wheelhouse. It had been twisted and bent by the forces of nature, shattering the middle section and leaving the bow and stern decks titled in opposite directions. Despite its age and condition, it had obviously been taken care of before its unfortunate demise. The hull was painted a medium blue, the deck varnished to a deep gold and the wheelhouse was yellow and white. The name of the ship was just visible where the bow had been driven into the sandy soil. It was called 'Sally's Inheritance' which he supposed was a joke name, although he didn't suppose Sally found it very funny, at least not now. It had probably broken free of its moorings during a storm, but there was no indication of where it had come from.

Because of the damage and the hull being partially buried, the open doorway which led into the wheelhouse was only a few feet above the sand. Terry stopped suddenly when he reached it, then carefully leaned inside to look around. He straightened up and took a step backwards before turning to the others and retracing his steps, his face serious.

Dawn immediately noticed. "What's wrong?"

They all turned to face Terry, their smiles fading when they saw his expression.

"There's a tripwire across the door. It's linked to a weight that pulls the triggers of two flare guns, one pointed towards the door, one aimed straight up through a hole in the roof."

"Why would they do that?" Jenna gasped. "People come here sometimes."

"It's for us," Ryan said seriously.

"They don't know us, or that we were coming here," Dawn said, grabbing Terry's hand.

"No, not us personally, but the people who have ruined their plans for the last three years."

"So, us then," Jenna said.

"Yes. I know what you mean, Ry," Conner said. "They don't know it was us, but they know someone might come snooping around. That's what the trap is for. One flare to show we're here, one flare to injure someone so they can trace us through the hospital if we escape."

"That's horrible!" Dawn said.

"Yeah. Looks like the Kneasleys are getting upset with us," Ryan said.

"So, do we leave it or disable the trap?" Conner asked.

"If we disable it they'll know someone's been here," Terry said. "Besides, it's a bit risky messing with live flare guns that someone else has set up. Then again, if we leave it an innocent tourist might get injured."

"Ok, how about this," Ryan said. "We hide somewhere we can see, set off the trap with a branch or something and then see if anyone turns up. They'll think it was an accident and we're in the clear."

They all nodded. "Great idea."

"Could take a while," Conner said. "Unless whoever was in the speedboat is waiting out there ready to rush back."

"What if they saw us and deliberately let themselves be seen?" Dawn said.

"Then they know or suspect we're involved, which is a frightening thought," Jenna replied.

"Right, so we have no choice," Conner said decisively. "If they know it was us, as in "us" personally, they'll be here quickly. If they know it's someone but don't know it's us, they probably won't be here quickly. Does that make sense?"

"Clear as mud, Con," Ryan smirked.

"I get it," Dawn said.

"Right, let's move the boat and set up a base. We've got all our camping stuff, so it doesn't matter how long it takes."

They retraced their steps as carefully as possible and climbed back into the 'eggy Su'. Terry got in last after making sure they hadn't left any distinctive footprints in the soft sand. "The waves will wash away the mark the 'eggy Su' made. I think the footprints we left are lost among the others. I don't think anyone but the bald guy knows how to read spoor anyway, so we should be fine."

"What if it is the bald guy?" Jenna asked.

"We should still be fine. Someone landed, walked around the beach and left. There's nothing that leads to us."

They moved to the leeward side of the island and found another beach, this one mostly shingle. It was close enough to the shipwreck beach to walk to, far enough away to not be noticed unless someone came looking. They moored the 'eggy Su' as close in as they could, but being white it was quite visible if someone was looking hard enough. Terry found a few strands of dead kelp on the beach and draped it over the hull, breaking up the outline a little. It wasn't perfect but was better than nothing.

"Ok, if a lot of people show up, we get out of there, as fast as we can. If it's just one or two people we stay long enough to get pictures, then run, ok?" Conner suggested.

They all agreed and set off for the beach. The island was relatively low, only about twenty yards above sea level at its highest point. At the southern end, it was less than a quarter of a mile across; so it didn't take them long to reach a point overlooking the shipwreck. Terry went forward while the others hid in a suitable spot behind and beneath some low but thick bushes. The ground was dry and sandy and there were few insects, no snakes or other natural hazards to disturb or force them to move.

From there, the others watched Terry stealthily approach the wreck and then search around for something to use. He found an old piece of timber that had fallen off the wreck and moved a few yards from the doorway. With a quick glance up at their hiding place, he made a thumbs up sign; making sure he wasn't in the line of fire, he threw the wood onto the tripwire.

The trap went off immediately. There were two soft bangs and two balls of flame went shooting from the wreck. One shot out of the door and along the beach, landing with a sizzle in the ocean. The other shot high into the air and exploded with a loud bang. Everyone within a wide distance would have seen or heard it.

Conner groaned. "I just realised the flaw in our plan."

"What?"

"Anyone who sees the flare could turn up, not just the Kneasleys' goons."

"Possibly, but most people will just report it to the Coast Guard, not show up themselves." Dawn pointed out. "It's not exactly busy out here."

"Let's hope so."

"Besides, that makes sense. The Coast Guard or someone else turns up and takes the injured person to hospital, which makes the local news, and the Kneasleys know who and where we are."

"Yeah, true."

Jenna patted Conner on the arm. "We had to set it off, we couldn't have just left it to hurt someone."

"True," Conner brightened. "Ok, let's see who shows. I bet you a 16-inch meat feast it's the tennis coach."

"That's not much of a bet, your parents own a pizzeria," Ryan pointed out.

"I don't just get free pizza whenever I want."

"Yes, you do!"

Conner smiled broadly and nodded. "Yes, I do."

Terry returned after taking a wide circle away from the bushes so he didn't leave a trail. "I can hear you talking from right down there," he whispered. "Remember, the human voice is very distinctive and can be heard a long way off, particularly by other humans."

"Sorry," they whispered in return.

Keeping hidden as much as possible, Terry and Ryan scanned the area, Terry with his eyes and Ryan with his binoculars.

"There's a ship, a trawler, in the distance. I didn't think there were any of them left working," Ryan said. "I think it's moving away from us. Can't see anything else except a couple of sailboats near the coast."

"How long do we give it?"

"A couple of hours," Conner said. "That speedboat is fast and could easily get here by then."

Only a few minutes later the distinctive sound of a helicopter was heard and the aircraft appeared as a speck in the distance. It flew towards the island and was soon revealed as a Coast Guard helicopter with its distinctive white and red paintwork. The teens stayed hidden under the bushes, each feeling guilty about what was actually a false alarm. The helicopter flew around for a while, occasionally hovering before moving on. At one point, the down draft of its rotors shook the bushes the teens were hiding under. They thought they'd been spotted, but only a few seconds later the chopper slid out over the sea, headed north and faded from sight and hearing. Silence fell on the island except for the gentle waves hitting the beach and the distant cry of a gull.

Once it was all clear, Terry returned to the wreck and checked the trap, being careful not to leave any extra footprints. He noticed a sharp chemical smell blowing on the wind as he approached. The trap had worked as intended and both flare guns were now disarmed and couldn't hurt anyone. The piece of timber Terry had used was sitting on the deck on top of the thin wire they'd used to set the trap. The rock weight had hit the deck and rolled into a corner. Satisfied it looked like an accidental triggering, and leaving everything in place for now, he returned to the others to report the good news.

CHAPTER TWO

NEW FACES

PIPE DOWN

Current usage:
Quiet down, stop making so much noise.

Original use:
The Bos'n would blow a certain tune on his pipe to release the deck crew from their duties and go below to rest.

As time went on and nobody else appeared, on the water or in the air, the stakeout turned into more of a picnic. An hour later nothing had happened. They chatted quietly and played games on their phones, with the sound off. After two hours Terry looked up from his screen and listened, lifting his head slightly and turning it slowly. The others also stopped what they were doing and waited for him to speak.

"There's a boat coming from the south. Outboard engines and very powerful, could be the red speedboat."

Soon after, Terry was proved correct when the boat they'd seen during last year's adventure appeared. It had no name or other markings and had been driven by a tall, thin man they called the tennis coach because of the way he dressed or sometimes by a shorter bald man who seemed to be something of a tracker. This time it was the tennis coach, dressed in a sky-blue shirt and white shorts. He was an excellent boatman, approaching the shore at some speed then dropping the throttle into reverse and stopping with the bow gently touching the sand close to the shipwreck. He killed the engine and looked around without getting out, then spoke into his radio. He might have been good with boats, but when it came to stealth, he was terrible.

"Marty! You there?" he said loudly.

The radio crackled and someone spoke. The man turned up the volume and said, "say again!"

The speaker crackled a little and Marty asked, "did we get anyone?"

"Nope, nothing here, looks like something fell across the tripwire, a piece of wood or something."

"Damn. Ok, leave it, we're done with the place anyway. Any sign of the Coast Guard?"

"Nope, nobody here but me."

"Ok, good. Do a quick check then head straight back here quick as you can."

"Will do."

The man put the radio mic down, switched off the radio and leaned back, stretching out his long legs and resting them on the dash. He was indeed wearing tennis shoes, bright white ones with matching socks. The teens watched quietly as he seemed to fall asleep. About 25 minutes later, he twitched his whole body and woke himself up. He sat up and looked around as if puzzled by where he was. Then he rubbed his eyes, stretched, and finally started the outboard. In no particular hurry, he reversed away from the beach, turned north, then suddenly pushed the engines to full throttle and sped away with a 'whoop!'. Only a few minutes later he was gone, leaving another wake and the rapidly fading sound of the outboard.

The teens cautiously emerged from their hiding place and looked around, Terry first.

"All clear," he whispered.

"Let's have a quick look around the shipwreck and then get out of here," Conner said.

"And clean up those glass bottles, we don't want them smashed up in the sand for someone to stand on," Jenna said.

"We should get some radios, for when we're out of range of the cell towers," Ryan said. "One each would be ideal, but even a pair would be useful."

"A satellite phone would be more useful," Conner replied, "although they might be out of our price range."

"A couple of old walkie-talkies are out of our price range," Dawn pointed out.

"We might be able to manage a few cheap ones," Ryan insisted. "We'd get good range out here, a few miles at least. Less on an island or ashore. I'll look into it."

"Do you think we could track Marty from his radio signal?" Conner asked.

"Probably, with the right kit, which we don't have and can't afford."

"And he's probably on Nic's trawler anyway, which is usually moored at Eagle Bay."

Ryan laughed, "yeah, he's not the most difficult person to find."

They followed Terry down to the shipwreck and began to gather up the bottles while he checked that there were no more traps and went inside the wreck. A few minutes later he emerged, holding something in his hand. "There's nothing interesting inside now, but something was definitely going on in there. The floor is scuffed in four equal places as if they had a table or bench set up. And there are new holes in the wood all over, as if they had things nailed up. Someone has done a good job of taking it all down and clearing it out. The only thing they left behind was these." He opened his hand to reveal several short pieces of clean white thread. He handed them to Dawn, who was the unofficial keeper of such things. "They weren't caught on anything, just lying loose in a corner."

"Not cotton," she said testing one of the longer pieces. "Too strong. Nylon maybe."

"So, they cut something up," Conner said.

"A fishing net?" Ryan guessed.

"Maybe, never seen a white fishing net though," Dawn said, wrapping the threads in a page torn from her notebook.

"I hate this part," Jenna sighed. "Too many questions and not enough answers."

Ryan grinned widely, "I love this part. All the mystery and suspense, not knowing what's going to happen next. And we've only just started."

"Should we take the flare guns?" Conner asked.

"I think we should leave them," Terry suggested. "There's a chance they could come back, and that would show them someone was here."

"Yeah, makes sense."

"Listen, we need to be more careful this time around," Terry said. "I mean it. This kind of trap was designed to hurt somebody. Who knows what else they have planned. Let's think twice before we act, and not just go running in."

The others nodded seriously. Then they raced over the hill and back towards the 'eggy Su', Ryan just beating Jenna, Conner a few seconds behind. Dawn and Terry ran hand in hand, finishing joined last. Once the 'eggy Su' was launched and they were safe from being overheard, they talked about what had happened.

"Looks like we just missed whatever was going on here," Dawn said, scrolling through her notes. "Maybe even by only a few days, which is frustrating."

"More importantly, it looks like they don't know who we are, and the trap was a long shot." Terry said.

"And who is this Scott person he mentioned?" Dawn asked. "He's a new character."

"No idea, unless it's the bald guy, we don't have a name for him yet," Terry replied.

"Possibly. I wonder why he needed checking up on, and where is he?"

"The tennis coach headed north, so somewhere up that way I'd guess."

"I wonder where they've all moved to?" Conner was steering them across open water, heading for Stonehaven Harbor on the mainland, which was visible as a dark smudge on the horizon. "I hope we don't have two places to stake out." He'd done this journey so many times he barely thought about what he was doing.

Jenna sighed, "I suppose we'll have to go looking for them, like we did last year."

Ryan, who everyone thought was asleep, spoke. "Let's be smarter this year. We can follow Marty from the marina, he's always led us to where the action is."

They all agreed it was a good idea.

"But not tonight, I have a date." Ryan grinned.

"Me too!" said Dawn with a laugh.

"Me three." Terry grinned.

"Yeah, I've got to call my boyfriend in D.C." Jenna added.

"Great. And I'm just going to help my parents in the pizzeria," Conner sighed. "Chopping onions and slicing salami while you all have fun."

Ryan turned around and smirked. "Oh, and is Erica working tonight by any chance?"

"Shut up, Ryan!" Conner hissed.

The other's all turned to look at him.

"Who's Erica?" Dawn asked, trying not to smile.

"She's one of the servers, she just started a few weeks ago."

"Is she pretty?" Jenna asked.

"I think so," Conner answered.

"Well, that's all that matters."

"Have you asked her out yet?" Dawn asked.

"No."

"Well, if you don't ask her out, she won't know you want to take her out."

"I know that, but if I ask her and she says no, I will have to keep working with her."

"You don't work there full time, and besides, how else are you going to know?"

"She might ask him out," Ryan grinned. "Stranger things have happened."

"Just . . . shut up. I'll do it my way."

They could see Conner was getting upset so they changed the subject. Soon after, they arrived back in the harbor, mooring up in their usual spot on the wooden jetty. Situated at the northern end of town, the harbor was a simple L shaped wall made from local stone cut from the now closed Stonehaven quarry. The short arm butted against a solid quay on which sat a two-story structure which contained the Harbormaster's office and other facilities provided for the local fishermen. This place was supposed to be a working harbor; but there was no sign of any activity today. It was once filled with trawlers and shrimp boats, but falling fish stocks had ruined the industry locally. Now, the only fishing trips were on tourist vessels converted from those ships, and all the pleasure craft were moored in the clean and not at all smelly marina on the southern edge of Stonehaven.

Taking Terry's advice about being more careful, the teens talked about their plans for the evening, computer games they wanted to play and generally anything that wasn't about what they'd found on Crow Head Island. It was unlikely anyone was listening, but better to be safe than sorry. They still took their usual route home through Stonehaven, between the stores and high-rise apartment blocks. The town was very touristy near the sea and residential away from it. Somewhere in the middle the two aspects blended together. In winter, the town was only a little different: less people on the streets, less traffic on the roads, and fewer lights in the windows of the expensive apartments with sea views.

The teens knew almost every inch of the place, every short cut and alley, every backstreet and main road. Almost without thinking, they took the shortest route. They were almost halfway home before they remembered they were supposed to be careful, and began to vary their route. This took a little longer but they were in no hurry. They had no choice in their destinations of course, and soon they split up and headed to their own homes. Almost as soon as they parted, the text messages began to flo as if they hadn't just spent the entire day together.

Early the next morning, the teens had assembled at the harbor and were now headed to the marina on the southern edge of town. The sea was light and a cool wind was blowing off the ocean, taking some of the heat out of the sun shining from a cloudless sky. Few tourist boats were out at this time of day, but that would soon change.

"We never did get that solar panel," Ryan said, "we could have been in the shade now if we'd fitted it as a roof."

Jenna turned around to look at Ryan. "I thought you had one?"

"Yeah, I did. I swapped it for a better battery control unit."

"So, you've only got yourself to blame then?"

"We did need a new controller to charge faster. I'm sure we can get another panel from somewhere." Conner twisted the throttle a little more to increase their speed. "Is that cooler?"

"Yes, for now."

They soon arrived at the marina, Conner slowing them down to a more suitable speed as they entered. The largest ships were moored near the entrance; expensive multi-deck yachts with gleaming chrome and smoked glass windows, all with immaculate white paintwork. Next came the smaller ships, then the speed boats and cabin cruisers, and finally the tiny rowing boats and kayaks, tucked away out of sight. As the tide was out, Conner was able to slip the boat around most of the jetties and approach this area without being seen.

There was no sign of the red speedboat, but they soon spotted Marty Whitford's old boat, a tiny two-seater with a rusty outboard engine. It was supposed to be white, but time and neglect had rendered it grey and green. A short scout around revealed Marty, and his buddy Nic, standing around on the edge of the marina near an old but still solid shed with a faded sign on it. Most of the paint had been erased by the weather but they could make out the words 'Ships Chandlery' and the remnants of a phone number. Despite appearances, the store still seemed to be in business, a survivor from before the marina was built.

Terry hopped off the boat to look around and see if he could hear what Marty and Nic were talking about. He approached silently, taking a roundabout route not heading directly for them. The teens had bumped into Marty a few times, although Terry doubted he'd remember them. The last time they'd met face to face, Marty was unconscious after a drunken accident on Three Hills Island before the Kneasleys moved in. They'd saved his life by keeping him warm and towing his wrecked

RIB back to shore with him on it, something for which they were still awaiting a thank you. Terry noticed straight away that Marty had lost weight, his skin wasn't pale and sickly, and his hair was dyed a deep black. Nic was also a little slimmer and he'd also dyed his hair, a bright yellow-blonde that looked terrible. At least he'd be easy to spot. Both men were a similar height, around 5' 10", dressed in dark coloured waterproofs and laced-up military style boots. Terry watched them for a while as they wandered around near the chandlery, always staying close to it but never looking at them or any of the occasional customers. They were talking about football, their team had obviously lost and they were telling each other why and what the coaches should have done differently.

When it didn't look like they'd reveal anything useful, Terry sneaked back to the boat and told the others what he'd found.

"Ok, they're obviously here for something," Conner said, "let's wait and see what happens."

Only a short while later, a man and a woman arrived, walking down the hill from the direction of the marina parking lot. They were in their early thirties, both with brown hair and dressed in shorts and a vest. The man was wearing black sneakers and the woman purple sandals. They looked like people who'd just started their vacation, with tanned hands and faces and pale arms and legs.

Marty and Nic saw them coming and moved over to the side of the chandlery as if they were out of sight. The couple approached a little wearily and none of them offered to shake hands. There was a short conversation, mostly led by Marty, and the couple wandered off back towards the parking lot. Terry left the others to watch Marty while he and Dawn walked casually after them, hand in hand.

Shortly after, two more people appeared, with Terry and Dawn not far behind. This couple were middle-aged, walking arm in arm as if out for a stroll both wearing long pants and jackets, despite the heat. They also had a short meeting with Marty and Nic, then left. Terry and Dawn returned to the boat.

"Ok, both couples parked up in the parking lot." Dawn said. "I have their vehicle details and some pictures of them. We didn't recognize them or their cars."

"It looks to me as if they're recruiting," Jenna said.

"Yeah, could be," Conner replied. "But what for? None of them looked like goons or sailors."

"No, although appearances can be deceptive."

"True."

Marty and Nic returned to Marty's boat a few minutes after the second couple had left. It took several attempts to get the outboard going, then they headed out with a rasping engine and a cloud of thick gray smoke.

Conner slipped their boat out of hiding once Marty's boay was out of sight and followed the small boat, or at least the noise and a mobile cloud of smoke, as it turned south out of the marina. As they'd expected, the men headed for Eagle Bay a short way down the coast. On arrival, they carried on a short way up the Eagle River and moored up in a public spot, then went into a local bar.

"Well, we can't go in there," Ryan said. "So, what now? Do we wait until they come out, which will probably be a while, or something else?"

"I think they're done for the day," Jenna said. "That's their usual pattern."

"Yeah. Let's do an island run," Conner suggested. "From here we can head south to Battle Cove Island, then head north to Three Hills, taking in everything in between."

"Ok, sounds like a plan." Ryan slumped a little lower in his seat so he could sleep.

"Hey!" Conner nudged him. "You're on binocular duty."

"We aren't there yet." Ryan mumbled, not moving.

"What are we looking for?" Jenna said.

"Anything suspicious," Ryan answered quickly.

Jenna sighed. "Great, I love it when we have all the precise details."

"Well, that's Dawn's job," Ryan grinned, carefully not looking at his sister.

"Just look for a red speedboat, Jen, that's all I've got." Dawn sounded very disappointed.

By mid-afternoon they'd arrived back at Crow Head Island. Terry did a quick scouting trip but it was obvious nothing had changed.

"No one's been here but us; the trap hasn't been reset. So, what Marty said about them being done with the place looks to be true."

"The trail's gone cold then. I hate it when that happens," Jenna said.

"Looks like we'll have to go back to trailing Marty and Nic," Dawn sighed.

"Anything Ry?" Conner asked, as Ryan had been looking through his binoculars for a while.

"No. Just that trawler I saw. It has a patch of red at the front, I was just trying to read its name, but it's too far away. Seems to be heading north this time."

"It's a bit late to be starting anything now," Conner said. "Let's head back, do a quick tour of the marina and then call it a day."

The others agreed and they were soon on their way back to the marina. They didn't consider it a chore; they were silently skimming across the waves on a sunny day along the beautiful Maine coast. They were free, and carefree, at least for a while.

The marina was busy when they arrived, like it always was during the summer. From early morning to late at night, something was usually happening. When the late-night parties started to run down, the early morning fishermen would arrive. Then the pleasure boats would depart, returning in time for the parties to start, and it all went around again.

Conner followed several other boats in, all of them heading to their berths according to size. There was no sign of Marty or Nic, or anyone else who looked familiar when they arrived, and the chandlery was locked up tight.

"When one door shuts, another one slams in your face," Ryan said bitterly.

Conner took them around in a full circle and then steered them back out to sea, all of them on the lookout for anything out of place. They didn't find anything; it seemed the trail, what little they'd found, had indeed gone cold.

CHAPTER THREE
A STREAK OF RED

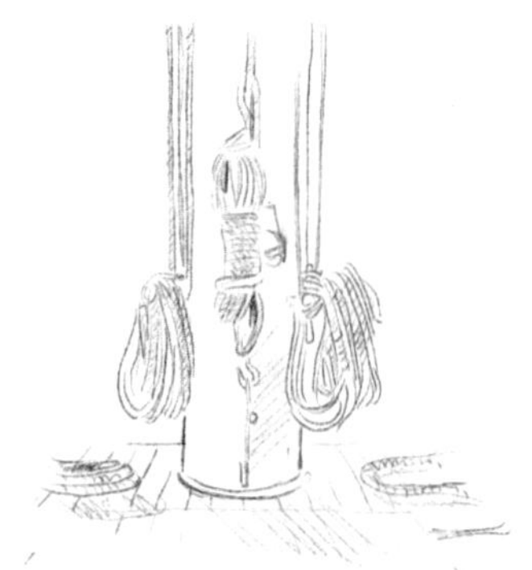

KNOW THE ROPES

Current usage:
To know the rules and/or procedures and traditions.

Original use:
Literally to know which ropes did what aboard a ship.
(There are over a hundred separate lines on a ship.)

The teens gathered in the harbor the next day, just sitting in the 'eggy Su' and chatting like they'd done before the academy had come along. Dawn, as usual was flicking through the notes on her phone. Conner had said nothing about what had happened with Erica, so the others avoided the subject of dating. They knew he'd tell them in his own time.

Dawn sighed. "I've been over this a hundred times and I only have one possible lead we could look into."

"One is better than none," Ryan said wisely.

"Yeah, what's the one? I've got nothing," Conner asked.

"It's not much, but we don't know anything about the red speedboat."

"Well, we have been looking for it, to be fair," Ryan said.

"Yes, looking for it generally, as we've been searching for clues," Dawn said. "But not directly. It has no name or registration, and we've never seen it moored up anywhere except when it was visiting. We've seen the tennis coach and the bald guy using it, but we don't know which one of them, if either, owns it. And we don't know who they are or where they live."

"That's true," Terry agreed. "And it's been involved in a lot of the stuff that's happened."

"If that's all there is, let's go," Jenna sighed.

"First, we have to find it, then hope it's the tennis coach using it and not the bald guy," Conner said. "he'll be much more difficult to follow."

"Let's head for the marina, we've seen it down there, and then try Three Hills," Conner suggested, preparing to leave. "There's always something happening there anyway." He twisted the throttle slightly and headed towards the harbor entrance, probably the only vessel that would do so today. Once out in the open sea he turned south and increased speed a little.

"Or we could listen out for the noise, it isn't exactly silent." Terry smiled.

"Can we try and be smart about the search?" Dawn asked. "We can't just go shooting wildly around all the islands in Maine and find it, at least not quickly."

"Good idea," Conner nodded, "what do we know about it?"

"It's got to be local," Ryan said, "those engines use a lot of gas so the range is limited and it seems to always be around the area."

"And as we haven't seen it moored up," Terry added, "it must be hidden or somewhere we haven't been."

"We've been almost everywhere around here, lots of times," Jenna said.

Dawn had pulled up a satellite map of the area and was zooming in and out. "We've pretty much covered the entire coast for miles around. It can't be moored on an island, it can't be up the river at Eagle Bay, unless it wasn't there when we were."

Ryan sat up, his eyes wide. "It's inside a ship, and they launch it when it's needed!"

Dawn sighed. "You watch too many spy movies."

"Wait, it could be inside something, maybe not a ship, but something," Terry said.

"Like a boathouse," Conner said. "There was one on Three Hills until the Kneasleys tore it down."

Dawn began scrolling around the map. "Ok, so a boathouse would need to be on land but near water, and it would probably be out of sight or at least not busy, because they want to keep it hidden."

"And not be seen when it leaves or goes back," Conner added.

"When we were on Crow Head Island the boat arrived from the south," Terry said, "I'm not sure but I think it always went that way when it left."

"Ok, let me see what's south," Dawn said. "Eagle Bay, too busy. Turtle Bay, nowhere to land there. We're assuming it would be on the mainland, so they can access it, yes?"

"Not necessarily, if they're hiding it, they could have two boats, one secret, one normal," Conner guessed.

"And it's got a radio," Ryan pointed out, "they could easily call it when it was needed, if it's in range. It can move fast enough to get here in a hurry."

"Wait, what's the range on that radio?" Dawn asked.

"Good point." Ryan nodded. "Hard to say. Better than a walkie talkie as it's mounted on a boat. Five to ten miles, in theory."

Dawn frowned. "Ok, I've got something; it fits most of what you said but it's a way south. Out of radio range."

"What is it?"

"Hawk Head Point. It's several miles south of Turtle Bay but it's a headland and it curves north, so not that far from Dead Man's Island actually." She turned her phone to show them, then zoomed in. "And right there, miles from anywhere . . ." The aerial photo showed a collection of small boats tightly clustered together inside a harbor wall.

"Is that a ship breaker?" Conner asked.

"Yep, according to this, it's a breaker and repair shop specialising in fast boats."

"Perfect place to hide a fast boat," Terry grinned.

"And it's on the mainland," Ryan pointed out. "They probably have cell phone reception, maybe even an old land line. No radio required."

Conner studied the photo for a few seconds, zoomed it out and then said, "Right, let's go."

They were a good way towards the marina by now, so Conner steered them away from shore and headed south, following the coast and the map in his head. At top speed, he took them past Turtle Bay, and further south until he could see the peninsula then turned slightly east to follow it around to Hawk Head Point.

"I don't think I've ever been this far south," Jenna said. "At least, not in a boat."

"Me neither," Dawn said.

"We came down here with our parents once Ry, Remember?"

"I think so. Did I catch a huge crab and it was running around the boat?"

"That's it."

"Was I there? I must have been very young."

"I don't really remember. You might have stayed with Gran. You were just a noisy kid back then."

"Thanks, bro," Dawn laughed.

Hawk Head Point came into view, and then patches of color where the boatyard was. Apart from the headland where a lighthouse stood, the land was much lower and flatter than they were used to. It mostly consisted of open grassland near the coast, heavily wooded further inland. There were a few other boats around and one of the converted shrimping ships that took tourists fishing was anchored in deeper water. Dozens of tourists were spread around the railings, hopefully casting the baited hooks that would probably never see a fish.

Conner took them towards the boatyard indirectly, getting close enough for Terry and Ryan to have a closer look.Ryan lifted his binoculars and looked out to sea, then around to the boatyard. "Wow, that place is a dump! I know it's supposed to be a breaker, but there's no breaking going on there, just rotting."

"Is it that bad?" Conner asked.

"Yes, a lot different from the satellite photo. All I see are old fiberglass hulls piled up with junk."

"Probably not going to be that easy; any sign of a red speedboat?" Dawn asked hopefully.

"Nope, I can't see anything that would float, never mind go that fast."

"Do you see anyone?" Conner said.

"No; but there are a few cars in the parking lot at the end of the access road, so someone might be inside. There's a large building made of stone, and some smaller ones leaning on it made from plywood and corrugated steel. The whole place looks run down."

"I suppose we could go in and look around, pretend we're customers."

"I'm not so sure," Terry said. "The 'eggy Su' is pretty distinctive. If there's anyone here involved with the Kneasleys, they'll be suspicious. They might report back to Marty, or be spooked enough to just go into hiding."

"They don't know our faces, we could walk in," Ryan suggested.

"Yes, good idea." Conner turned them towards the shore and headed closer in. "Is there anywhere we can land?"

Ryan scanned around, "Yeah, the whole area is low down. Looks like we can moor up almost anywhere. There are some fishermen on the rocks over there, and some kayaks on that shingle beach." Ryan pointed to the right of the boatyard.

Conner worked out where Ryan was pointing and headed towards an irregular cove a few hundred yards from the boatyard. He spotted the canoes and headed to one side of them, avoiding the area where the fishermen had cast their lines. A wide footpath led from the cove to the boatyard and beyond. It was overgrown in places, obviously never busy.

Conner expertly approached the rough shingle beach and nudged the 'eggy Su' into shore.

"I think someone should stay with the boat," Terry suggested, warily looking around.

"Ryan, you're it," Conner laughed.

"Why me? I thought I could be the muscle."

"You're the last one ashore, so today you're the boat guard."

"Ok, cool."

"And don't fall asleep."

"Ahh! Ok."

"And be ready to leave in a hurry," Terry whispered.

"Aye aye, no sleeping, fast getaway, got it."

The others leapt ashore as Ryan switched to the helm seat. They crunched up the beach and headed towards the boatyard. None of the people there paid them any attention. They soon arrived at the access road and walked casually towards the boatyard. There were only a handful of cars in the lot, one of which had a kayak rack on the top. A large motorbike was parked near the store.. It was old but the black body panels and chrome shone in the bright sun. A weatherworn sign across the front of the building read 'Seb's Boat Spares'. Underneath that was 'You Name It We Probably Got It'. It looked like any other store you'd find in a town, with two wide display windows and a central door.

Inside, the store was cleaner than they'd been expecting, although it wasn't very well stocked. To their left was a complete speedboat sitting in a simple wooden frame and angled slightly towards them. It was white, not red. To their right were several outboards, some intact, others in pieces. All of them were just lying on the floor with no thought for presentation.

There was no one around nor any bell to ring, so they headed through the store and emerged onto a wide concrete quay. Ryan's first impression of the place had been correct. It didn't look like there was a single working boat in the whole yard, and there certainly wasn't any breaking going on they could see. The yard smelled of the sea mixed with diesel and things slowly rotting away. There was no one out here either.

The teens had a quick look around the open area without much hope of finding the speedboat, then headed over towards one of the algae-covered plywood buildings marked 'workshop'. Just as they reached it a voice called out.

"Can I help you?" His tone didn't suggest he was very keen on helping them at all.

They turned around and were face to face with the bald man they'd seen with the tennis coach on their last adventure. He was wearing old but very clean blue coveralls and brown boots. There was a frayed 'S' on the left pocket but no other name tag, so they had no clue if this was Seb or only worked for him. With his hands tucked into his pockets and his shoulders back, he looked very unwelcoming. His expression didn't change as he examined them, so he was either an expert at hiding his feelings or he didn't recognize them.

"We were looking for an outboard, around 50hp," Conner said, thinking fast and trying to keep his voice light.

"Got nothing in at the moment," the man said without checking.

"Doesn't have to be a runner, just needs to have a good lower unit."

"No, nothing like that."

"Ok, thanks."

The man nodded and stood watching them as they went back into the store and moved to block the door so they couldn't come back. They exited the main door and stepped out onto the road, his glare still on their backs until they were out of sight. They didn't speak until they were back at the boat, trying to keep their expressions casual.

Conner laughed. "Wow, where did he go to customer service school?"

"I know, what a charming man," Jenna added.

"What happened?" Ryan asked eagerly "Did you find the speedboat?"

"No. Let's get going, we'll tell you when we're on the move."

Ryan had turned the boat side on the shore. Once they were all aboard, he turned and moved the 'eggy Su' slowly away from the shore.

Terry sat watching them until they noticed. "Seriously? You didn't see it?"

"The speedboat? No, just piles of junk."

"It was in the workshop."

"It was?" Dawn asked.

"Yes, on a boat trailer."

"How did you see it and we didn't."

"Because you were looking in the workshop and I was looking at the reflection in the water."

"It was definitely the one we're looking for?" Conner said.

"Red all over, no name or other markings, so almost certainly. I couldn't see the stern so I don't know about the big outboards. And that Seb guy was definitely the tracker we saw last year."

"If that was Seb," Dawn pointed out.

"Who's Seb?" Ryan asked.

"Well, the place is called Seb's Boat Spares, so it's possible that's the bald guy's name."

Ryan had moved them out to sea now and was slowly heading away from the boatyard."So what now? Wait around for them to make a move?"

Conner, who was sitting in Ryan's spot and itching to get back to the helm, said, "we don't have any other leads. Let's hang around for a while. We could break out the fishing rods."

They had some collapsible rods in the rope locker, which they took out and assembled. They didn't actually have any hooks, weights or bait, and only used them to make it look like they were fishing when they were on a stakeout at sea. With the motor turning slowly and the rods in position, the 'eggy Su' moved in a wide circle, the boatyard in view at all times. It was very peaceful with the low swell, a light breeze and the electric motor barely audible. It was the type of environment where you could easily fall asleep.

They were still circling by lunch time, so they lowered their rods and had a snack, bobbing on the waves. There were more boats around now, although it was nowhere near as busy as it was near Stonehaven, or even Eagle Bay. Low clouds rolled in from the sea and provided some shade. Darker clouds could be seen in the far distance, which the teens kept an eye on. The weather report hadn't forecast any storms, but it was a good idea to keep a watch on such things.

A short while later another boat approached the boatyard. It was a small white cabin cruiser, although not one they recognized. It appeared from the south, rounding the headland, its outboard motor rasping away. Ryan grabbed his binoculars and watched it go in. Seb caught something the occupant of the boat threw up to him, a small but heavy-looking package. They chatted for a few minutes then the boat left, heading south and back around the headland.

Only a few minutes later there was a roar of engines and the red speedboat appeared, much to Terry's delight. He looked around at the others but didn't speak. The speedboat, as they suspected, headed north, with what looked like Seb at the wheel. From experience, they knew he wasn't as good a boatman as the tennis coach but was more aware of his surroundings and harder to sneak up on.

With a quick swap around, Conner took his place at the helm and they set off in pursuit. They kept the speedboat on the edge of disappearing from sight behind the waves, the noise of the engines still clear. The speedboat approached a distinctive island, a column known as Gull Rock, and slowed almost to a stop. They could no longer hear the sound of the engines and only just about make out a flash of red as the waves lifted the 'eggy Su'.

"I think Seb's checking if he's being followed," Terry said.

Conner turned slightly so they weren't heading directly towards him, keeping up their previous speed. A few tense moments crawled by, then the engines roared again. The speedboat moved east at a slower speed then looped around to the south and then suddenly turned north again.

"What is he doing?" Conner hissed.

"He might have spotted us but not know if we're following him," Terry guessed. "Just keep your speed and heading, let's see what he does."

The speedboat slowed again, turned towards the east and suddenly increased its speed to maximum.

"Ok, go," Terry said. "I think he goes full speed when he's feeling confident."

Conner eased them back on course and set off after the speedboat, easily able to keep up.

"I wish we could race him; I think we'd take him easy," Ryan bragged.

"Not now, Ry, we've got more important things to do."

Soon, another familiar island appeared ahead.

"Dead Man's Island dead ahead." Conner grinned.

"Very good Con, but dad jokes at your age?"

"Hey, that was funny."

"I'm surprised they're going back there after last year," Jenna said.

"Well, they burnt all the evidence, including the shipping container, so I doubt the authorities will still be interested," Dawn said.

The engine noise faded as they saw a red flash go around the other side of the island. Conner changed course to keep the large island between them and the speedboat and slowed down. They were on the western side of the landmass and knew there was a landing place, called Battle Cove, on the eastern end. It faced out towards the open sea and was just a strip of rock and a small cave, now burnt black inside. Very few people went there, so it made a good meeting place.

Conner moved closer to the island with the intention of mooring up in the split in the rock they'd found last year. It was hidden from view and a secure place to leave the 'eggy Su'.

Seconds later the speedboat shot out into the open sea and headed south at some speed.

"Should we follow?" Conner said backing away from the island.

"Let's see if we can find out what he came here for," Terry suggested.

Conner headed south, hugging the coast in case someone else appeared. Another noise reached their ears, the deep thrum of an inboard diesel engine. It was coming from the cove as far as they could tell. Conner headed towards the sound, stopping just before they would become visible to whoever was there. With small blips of the throttle, he inched closer to the cove. They rounded the rock in time to see a trawler heading north at full speed, which was relatively slowly.

"Is that the trawler you saw, Ry?" Conner asked.

"Not sure, go around, I need to see the bow."

Conned moved backwards out of sight, then turned and headed around the island, keeping it between them and the trawler. By the time they reached the other side, the trawler was some distance away. Ryan raised his binoculars and examined the ship.

"Yes, that's it, red stripe at the front. Unless there's two the same, that's the one I saw."

"Ok," Jenna said, "but what is it doing, certainly suspicious, I suppose. Nothing illegal though."

"Somebody delivered something to Seb, something urgently needed by the trawler. So, he brought it out here." Dawn said, tapping away at her screen. "That's not normal behaviour. I think the trail just got a bit warmer."

"And bigger, I don't think we can miss a trawler." Ryan smirked.

"Should we follow, the battery isn't too low," Conner asked the others.

"Personally, I need a comfort stop," Terry said. "We can find the trawler easily enough tomorrow. We'll have no trouble keeping up with it."

"Agreed," Dawn said.

"Ok, I'll take us back to the harbor."

"Right, let's have some guesses," Conner said to distract them as they headed home. "What are they smuggling?"

Ryan thought for a few seconds. "Ok, the white cabin cruiser brought some fake passports for the trawler crew, who are all spies and international assassins. Seb delivered them then got out of there because he was scared of them."

"Dawn?"

"I think my brother watches too many videos online, and Seb was delivering a spare part for the trawler's engines."

"Boring," Ryan whispered.

"Jenna?"

"I think we don't have anywhere near enough information to make a guess, but I'm going to anyway because Ryan will be upset if I don't. I'm just going to say 'drugs'."

"No, I won't," Ryan insisted quietly.

"Terry?"

"When you watch the news, you sometimes see drug raids and there's huge packages of the things, so I don't think it's that. I'm going to say diamonds, small and easily smuggled but with a high value."

"Yeah, good guess!" Conner said. "I'm going with technical plans, like schematics for building some kind of technology, stored on a portable data storage device of some kind."

"Like a laser death ray, or a huge killer robot, yeah, that's cool," Ryan added.

"What do we win?" Dawn asked.

"Err, pizza?"

"What if you win?"

"Still pizza, but you all pay for it."

CHAPTER FOUR

A RAY OF LIGHT

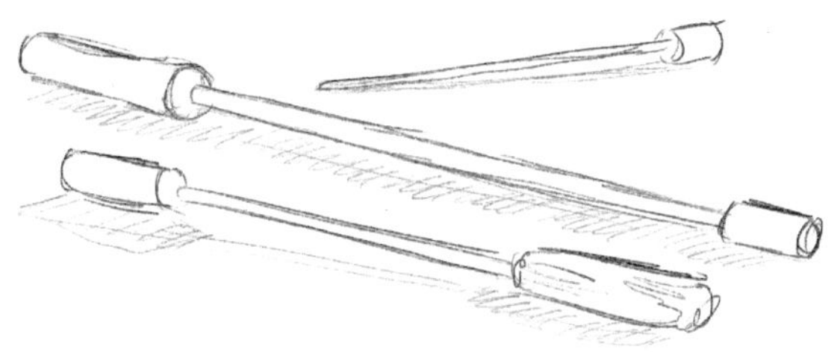

AT LOGGERHEADS

Current usage:
To go head to head in a negative way,
to disagree when both sides being stubborn.

Original use:
A loggerhead was a tool for smoothing out the tar in the deck seams. It had a shaft with a shaped metal weight at the end and was used for discipline as well as decks!

The next morning found them up early and well on their way before most people had got out of bed. They soon arrived at Rogue Island, site of the Maritime Academy, they were the first students. It was owned and run by Frank F. Herresat, also known as the Boat Prof.

Ryan and Conner had started a small business converting outboard motors to electric, with the occasional help from Dawn, and the others when they were there. Their skills weren't greatly in demand at the moment, but it brought in some extra money to allow them to maintain and upgrade the 'eggy Su'.

Most of their time here had been spent working on a small yacht the Boat Prof had given them. It had been almost buried in mud when they'd first seen it, and they were convinced it was only fit for firewood. After digging out the pieces, and making new ones where necessary, the yacht was nearly finished. The only thing it lacked was a mast. The teens assumed they'd need to find a suitable tree to cut down and shape the trunk to fit. They were all very surprised to learn they could actually make a mast from lengths of timber; it could be hollow to save weight and still be strong enough.

They gathered in the wood shop, where the mast was standing on trestles, all ready to go. They just needed to lift it into place.

"If they aren't on any of the islands, where are they?" Ryan asked, running his hand along the smooth timber.

"They might have moved inland," Dawn said. "Maybe we annoyed them too much and they've moved elsewhere."

"The Kneasleys are still on Three Hills," Ryan pointed out, "and if they're still around they're up to something."

Jenna smiled. "A few years ago, I'd have laughed at you for saying that. Now, I'm not so sure." She quickly added, "although I'm not 100 percent convinced that they're up to something right now."

"I am," Ryan insisted.

The teens fell silent when they heard footsteps. They stepped outside and were suddenly surrounded by dogs of every size and kind. They made a big fuss of them all, Ryan favouring Chain, the Doberman cross who had tried to attack Ryan last year, but who they'd charmed with food. She'd put on weight and was looking like a normal dog now, which is more than could be said for the others, who all had a piece missing.

Accompanying the dogs was the Professor himself, a retired Royal Navy captain by the name of Nathaniel Clifton, and a woman around the Prof's age. The Professor, or Boat Prof, was in his mid-sixties, with short gray hair and sharp blue eyes. As usual, he was clean shaven, had heavily tanned skin and a rosy glow to his cheeks. He was wearing a coverall that had once been white but were now covered in paint, oil and glue. On his feet were military-style high boots with no laces.

Nathaniel, who liked to be called Nat, was in his late fifties, had a neat black beard and was mostly bald with a few black patches on the sides of his head. He was wearing a neat white shirt, formal trousers, a blue blazer and red Wellington boots. It was easy to tell he was British what with his attire and his accent.

Once they'd disentangled themselves from the dogs, which wasn't easy, the Prof introduced the new arrival.

"Hello all. I'd like to introduce you to Betty Quansah, our newest faculty member. She's an expert on metal fabrication, welding techniques, and, unfortunately, internal combustion engines." The Prof laughed.

Betty smiled widely, showing a gold tooth among the white. "Hey, they aren't finished yet!"

She was about the same height as Dawn, about 5 feet 4, her dark skin was almost black, her hair was black and her eyes were a deep brown. She was wearing what looked like a brand-new blue coverall and stout black boots. She sounded Australian. "Good to meet you, the Prof has told me all about you." She shook hands with them all; her skin soft from her aloe lotion.

"Nice to meet you, Betty," Jenna said. "Where are you from?"

"I was born in Ghana, if you know where that is?"

"West Africa," Dawn answered, "on the Atlantic coast. Capital city is Accra."

Betty smiled warmly. "I'm impressed. I didn't stay there long though. I grew up at sea really, spent a lot of time around the Australian coast, as you can probably tell. It's where I met this bloke." She gestured with her thumb towards the Prof.

With greetings exchanged and the dogs fussed again, the humans began preparations to install the mast in the yacht and the dogs ran off to do doggy stuff. As masts went, theirs wasn't the largest or heaviest but it still had to be lifted up and lowered into place in the special socket designed for it. For the most part, the adults let the teens work it out. They held ropes and acted as counterweights while the teens worked through the problem. Betty had produced a huge pair of leather gauntlets from somewhere, which explained her very soft hands.

In the end, they decided to launch the yacht, moor it in the harbor, and then use the height difference between the land and the sea as the coaxial. With a rope and pulley system rigged to the wind turbine tower, the mast was soon fixed in place and the yacht was almost finished.

A cheer went up as the Prof ceremonially handed over a kitbag with the sail and rigging inside. "Ok, last step. We'll leave you to it. Shout if you need help."

"Good luck!" Nat smiled.

"Have fun!" Betty added with a wide smile.

As the adults walked away, Conner opened the bag and tipped the contents out on the deck. The teens stood around looking at it for a few moments, and then began to spread it out to see what they had. Conner then pulled out the old copy of the maritime book he carried everywhere. It was written by the Prof himself many years ago, but the knowledge was still relevant. He found the right page and studied the diagrams. The others gathered around and they soon worked it out. They only had to take it all down twice before it was finally done. The pristine white sail flapped in the gentle breeze, making the familiar sound.

"Ok, we need a name," Conner said.

"Also, we need an anchor," Ryan pointed out.

"That's a strange name for a boat," Conner grinned.

"Well, we have the–officially–Peggy Sue, so something similar?" Dawn said.

"Nah, let's be different," Ryan insisted. "The Electric Eel!"

"It's not electric," Dawn pointed out.

"It will be when I've finished with it. We need a motor to move it around when the sail's down or there's no wind."

"Why don't we go with something from nature?" Terry suggested. "Like a fish or a bird."

"Yes, I like that," Dawn grinned.

"Something that's native to this coast," Jenna added.

Dawn smiled. "Research time!"

For the rest of that day and the day after, the Prof took the teens out and taught them to sail. It was a small yacht with only one sail, so it wasn't too complicated. They all had trouble grasping the concept of sailing against the wind, but they finally got the hang of it. No one was surprised that Conner was the best sailor; he'd always had a natural skill with boats. Betty lent the teens a small outboard motor from her personal collection. It was tiny and looked like the dough mixer in the pizzeria, but it worked fine, even though it had a gasoline engine. It reminded them of the engine the 'eggy Su' had originally, although this one ran smoothly and didn't make as much noise or smoke. Still, it was a gas engine, and they vowed to use it as little as possible and replace it with an electric version as soon as they could.

Once he was satisfied that they knew what they were doing, the Prof let the teens take the boat out alone. He knew they were sea-smart and wouldn't do anything to put themselves in danger. Conner, who seemed to be in charge of such things, transferred the emergency flares and the oars from the 'eggy Su'. They all piled in and took their usual places out of habit.

The boat was an unusual design, about 21 feet long, with a sharp prow. It was somewhere between a sailing dinghy and a day-sailor. There were four thwarts; the one at the prow requiring anyone sitting on it to face backwards. There was storage up front but no cabin. The design allowed the boat to be controlled by a single person, if they were experienced. As they weren't yet up to that, Conner steered the boat with the curved tiller while Ryan and Dawn worked the sail. Jenna and Terry were on lookout duty. Later, they all swapped places, sailing in almost perfect silence around Rogue Island. Once they'd all gained some confidence, and with Conner back at the tiller, they moved away from the island and tried to find some better wind to see how fast it could go. Although it was quieter even than the 'eggy Su', the yacht was nowhere near as fast even with a good wind on the open sea.

Conner was practising his tacking, moving the boat against the wind by taking a zigzagging course. This made the journey even slower as they had to cover twice the distance. Conner had a new-found respect for the old sailing ship crews by the time he'd had enough.

As they were heading back to Rogue Island, Terry spotted something in the distance. "Is that a trawler over there? Might be the one we saw the speedboat meeting up with."

Ryan lifted his binoculars and looked to where Terry was pointing. "I see it. Yes, that's the one I saw before, with the red at the front. It doesn't seem to have any nets out though."

"That's strange," Dawn said casually.

Ryan turned to look at her, his eyes wide. "No, that's suspicious!"

"We need to investigate it, but not in this," Conner said. "We're too slow and too easy to see with this white sail high above the water."

"Ok, let's go back and get the 'eggy Su' and then come back and find it."

"Not sure we can do that today; it will be too late by the time we get back to the academy and then back here with the 'eggy Su'.

"Yeah, ok. I'm sure we'll be able to find it again."

Ryan kept his binoculars trained on the strange trawler until it disappeared behind an island. It seemed to be moving at a good speed, certainly too fast for trawling.

It took them two hours to get back to the academy harbor, Conner having to tack against an offshore wind for most of the journey. The teens made the most of it, relaxing and enjoying the sound of the gentle waves and the wind flapping the sails.

The next morning, with all their kit transferred back to the 'eggy Su', the teens set off again. The yacht was great, they decided, but for investigating suspicious trawlers only the 'eggy Su' was good enough. Ryan had examined the charts the previous evening and checked the approximate positions he'd seen the trawler before. They had some idea of its direction from their sighting yesterday. The information they had was sparse, as Jenna pointed out, and all they could really tell was the ship seemed to stay around the outer islands.

All they could do is go and look for it again. At least it was big and fairly easy to spot from a distance. Conner turned then towards where they spotted it yesterday and headed off at top speed. Ryan almost had the binoculars glued to his face, which wasn't unusual, while Terry used his natural vision. There was no sign of the trawler anywhere around where they'd seen it, so Conner turned them north, the direction it was last seen traveling.

"That's Crow Head Island," Terry pointed to the grey smudge they were approaching.

"Coincidence? I think not," Ryan said dramatically.

Jenna laughed and rolled her eyes. "If the trawler is sailing up and down and around the islands it will pass them all eventually, so yes, coincidence."

"I'll bet you a calzone it's not."

"Ry, stop gambling with my parents' pizzas."

"It's ok, I'll pay for it. Anyway, you do it all the time."

"Well, they're my parents."

"If we assume they're up to something," Dawn said sternly, a blank page open on her phone, "what is it. What can they do on a trawler?"

"All kinds of things," Ryan said. "I mean, probably not dentistry, not while the ship's moving, but lots of other things."

"If we also assume it's the Kneasleys," Terry said without taking his eyes off the horizon, "then we can assume whatever they were doing in the shipwreck on Crow Head has been moved to the trawler, if the trawler is connected in any way to that or anything illegal."

Ryan tutted. "I wish people would stop being reasonable and logical and not jumping to conclusions, you're ruining it for me."

"That shipwreck didn't have anywhere near the same space as a trawler." Conner said. "If they had a table in there like you said, Terry, they must have room for a lot of tables. I they are up to something, it's a major operation."

"Thank Con, that's the kind of thing I want to hear."

"Can we all just keep an open mind," Jenna asked. "We have no evidence of anything at all at the moment. The only thing we have is the fact Marty and his goons planted a trap on Crow Head Island, and that's it really. We don't know anything about this trawler, it could just be a tourist ship."

"That's why we're investigating," Ryan said, looking at Jenna through the binoculars.

She couldn't help but smile at his antics. "Of course, we investigate and follow the evidence. Just like the scientific method."

"Great, we're all agreed."

They headed north for a while, then went back to Crow Head Island for a look around and a picnic lunch. Nothing had changed and no one had been here since. Ryan and Terry kept looking as they ate, then Ryan went to the highest point and used the binoculars to look all around. He could see plenty of boats from up here, including the huge cargo ships far out to sea. Closer to shore there were cruisers and speedboats and some windsurfers trying to catch the light breeze.

"There's something to the south-east. It was a flash of sunlight reflecting off something and I can see a tiny smudge of gray. It might just be one of the islands."

"We're heading south anyway, let's go and check it out," Conner said.

Making sure they'd left nothing behind, including footprints, they set off again, this time with more hope of finding the trawler. Even it if turned out to be an actual working fishing boat they would at least know it probably wasn't involved in anything illegal.

Time wore on and more islands came and went, some to port, some to starboard. Terry suddenly spotted something in the water. "What's that?" He pointed to starboard, a good distance from the boat and nothing the others could see. Ryan looked over to check.

"Yes, something. I think it's just a wake."

"Yes," Terry said patiently, "the wake of a ship."

Conner turned towards the island they were passing, which was Gray Island, a relatively small dome of rock covered in grass. No one lived there and very few people went ashore as there wasn't much to see. There was a large sandy spit at the northern end, which was completely underwater when the tide was in.

Now they were closer they could hear the sound of a diesel engine. It was just turning over not revving, presumably to drive a generator. The trawler soon came into sight, stern first, the wake fading now the propeller wasn't turning. Conner blipped the throttle into reverse to stop them then moved backwards out of sight.

"That's the one we've been seeing, right, Ry?" Conner asked.

"Yes, definitely. I've never seen a trawler around here with markings like that."

"Ok, I'll take us out in a wide arc and then work back towards it to get a better look."

Conner steered them away from the island and began racing around like they were tourists having fun. Each pass took them closer to the trawler. Ryan scanned the ship with his binoculars, trying not to reflect sunlight off the lenses.

He began to describe the trawler to the others. "Yes, that's what I saw. That red thing at the front is a wide stripe on the hull. Underneath it says 'Solar Ray" and under that "Ocean Research Vessel'. It's just an old trawler with a new paint job. There are no nets or fishing gear. And I can't see anyone on deck. They're really close to shore and that water is very shallow."

"Good thing Terry has sharp eyes, we nearly missed them." Dawn smiled warmly at him.

"Yes, good spot." Conner agreed. "I wonder what they're doing?"

"It says they're a research vessel," Jenna said, "they might have onboard instruments, or something in the water."

"Ok, I'm going to race up and down a bit longer; let's see if they move."

They all took turns at the motor and sped up and down and around in tight circles, always staying close enough to the trawler to see if anything happened aboard. After about an hour and with their battery getting low, the trawler fired up its main engines and began to move north. It didn't seem to be in any hurry, accelerating slowly and never going at top speed.

"I didn't see or hear it pull anything back aboard," Terry said. "So, if they had instruments deployed they must be towing them, which is possible."

"I'm telling you, it's just a cover." Ryan insisted. "We need to get on board and have a look, that thing is packed with smugglers, or something."

"Let's just research the "research" vessel before we do anything stupid," Dawn said. "If it's a proper research vessel someone will know about it."

"We could ask Aksel, he might know," Jenna suggested.

"Possibly, he did convert a trawler for research, so it would be a good place to start." Dawn started looking through her notes for mentions of Aksel and his vessel, the Sea Fox III. "They moved bases, but I have his email address."

Ryan nodded admiringly, "of course you do."

The teens followed the trawler as it headed north in an almost straight line. It didn't stop at the next couple of islands, nor seemed to be towing any instruments. Ryan, still looking through his trusty binoculars, spotted something. "Con, takes us around to the trawler's starboard side, I can see something, but I can't make them out."

Conner moved them around in an arc and then came back as Ryan had said. After a few moments he spoke. “Thought so. They have solar panels on the roof, quite a few of them, all different and lashed in place. Why do the need those if the ship is diesel powered?”

“Well, it is called the Solar Ray, maybe that’s why,” Dawn said.

“They’re probably fake, or not connected up,” Ryan was still looking through his binoculars. “Those trawlers have a decent generator for electrical power, they don’t need extra from solar panels.”

“Maybe the Kneasleys have gone green,” Conner said with a straight face.

The others laughed.

“If there’s a lot of equipment in there, the generator might not be enough,” Terry said.

“Possibly,” Ryan looked at him through the binoculars. “But what kind of equipment needs that kind of power?”

“One more thing to add to the mystery,” Jenna smiled at Ryan.

“Agree!,” Ryan replied, not sounding so cheerful this time.

The teens continued to follow the trawler at a distance. It didn’t stop at any of the islands, just sailed by them. Sometimes passing to the west, sometimes to the east, but always heading north. Dawn made plenty of notes but couldn’t see any pattern to the trawler’s movements. It was if the captain was out for a joyride and was weaving around the islands at random. They didn’t see anyone come out on deck, they didn’t drop any nets, or anything else. It was a complete mystery, and Dawn was very annoyed by it.

All their racing around earlier had used a lot of battery power and theirs was now very low. They had oars, but no one wanted to row all the way back to the harbor; they called off the investigation and headed for Stonehaven. Conner always kept some power in reserve, so they arrived safely. Once in range of a reliable internet signal, the teens hit their phones to see what they could find out about the converted trawler. Companies were rarely secretive about their worthy projects. The teens each had a message or two from their parents, which they quickly answered with as few words as possible. One advantage of being a little older this year was the decrease in parental overwatch.

CHAPTER FIVE

HUMAN NATURE

TRY A DIFFERENT TACK

Current usage:
Try a different approach or style
to find a solution to a problem.

Original use:
Ships could be on a port tack or a starboard tack.
Changing to the opposite tack might provide
a better course or more speed.

As time went on, their research into ships turned into other things. They were still young teenagers after all. Jenna, a competitive swimmer, was looking at some footage from the Olympics, Terry was playing a game, and Ryan was looking at solar panels. Conner was actually reading the Prof's maritime book, having scanned it into his phone page by page. Dawn, single-minded as ever, was doing the actual work.

"Ok, this could be useful. Ships Registry. Some data available to the public. Here we go, Solar Ray. Type; ocean research vessel, owners; a private company, 'RE:Search.' Wow, they really put some thought into that name. Wait, that looks familiar. We know someone with a company called ReKnew. I wonder . . ."

Mostly ignored by the others, Dawn continued her research and then sat back with a wide smile on her face. Only Terry paid any attention, and then not much. She waited patiently for them to notice and one by one they stopped what they were doing and looked over at her.

"Well, tell us then," Ryan insisted when she didn't speak.

She smiled wider. "The Solar Ray is owned by a private company. That private company is a subsidiary of another company, one you might recognize. ReKnew Recycling."

"I knew it!" Ryan shouted.

Even Jenna was impressed. "So, the Kneasleys are involved! Guess you were right, Ryan."

"Pretty obvious really, they're big fish in a small pond around here."

"I've also emailed Aksel, just waiting for a reply."

"And what now?" Conner asked. "They're up to something, we don't know what. The fact they're keeping it secret means it's probably illegal, but how do we prove it?"

"We'll have to get on that ship," Terry replied. "It will have to dock eventually, for fuel and supplies. We find out where it docks and sneak on then."

Dawn consulted her notes. "Its home berth is registered as Stonehaven. We've never seen it here or in the marina."

"Maybe it's down at Eagle Bay Harbor, we should take a run down there and see," Conner said.

"Possibly. It certainly can't fit in the harbor at Three Hills, or any of the other islands the Kneasleys have used," Terry pointed out.

"True." Conner nodded. "So, unless anything else turns up, we go to Eagle Bay, stake it out for a while. As Terry said, it's got to refuel somewhere, and take on food and water for the crew."

They headed home shortly thereafter. Ryan took the battery with him to recharge it. They had a small hand truck they used to transport it across town, which they left on the quay when they went out to sea. They were supposed to take it in turns to charge it, but Ryan was convinced the others were doing it wrong and had been taking sole responsibility for it. As batteries went, it was relatively small and only took a few hours to charge. Ryan had assured his parents the cost of the electricity used was quite reasonable.

The next day the hunt continued at Eagle Bay Harbor. Eagle Bay was the next town south of Stonehaven. It was built on either side of the Eagle River, although the bay had long since been filled in and built on. It was the kind of place people went for the day and was more touristy than Stonehaven, with more of the usual big-name brands. There was no harbor as such, despite the name. Instead, the trawlers moored up along a stone and concrete quay built along the north bank of the river. The few commercial boats that were left, the trawlers and shrimp boats, got the best spots nearest the entrance, then came the tourist boats, and then, quite a way up the river, the privately-owned craft.

The quay had been built wide enough to allow hand carts to move the crates of fish to the waiting delivery trucks. Now that the fishing industry was almost gone, it was being taken over for outdoor seating by many of the seafood restaurants, which imported most of their fish from elsewhere. The teens walked along the quay, blending in with the tourists, stopping occasionally at one of the many stores. They hadn't seen the Solar Ray when they'd arrived, so they decided to have a look around while they waited for it.

Even walking very slowly, they soon ran out of wharves to walk along. Instead, they sat on a bench and chatted quietly, with occasional glances out to sea. Several boats came and went, all tourist or private craft.

"You know what else is not here?" Dawn asked.

"What?"

"The Dark Cloud."

"Nic's trawler?" Ryan said. "Maybe he went fishing."

The others laughed at his joke. Marty Whitford's friend, Nic hadn't used his boat for its actual purpose since they'd first seen it.

"No, because that was its berth." Dawn pointed to where the Dark Cloud had been moored last year when they'd been here. Now, a shiny blue passenger boat was tied up there nose first, a short metal gangway resting on the quay.

"Wait," Dawn had a sudden thought. "What if the Dark Cloud is now the Solar Ray?" She pulled her phone out and tried to connect to the internet.

"Could be, they're the same type," Conner said.

"So Nic was having trouble like all the other fishermen and was forced to sell up?" Jenna said.

"Maybe, or he might have just sold it to someone else, or to a ship broker."

"Hmm. I was going to check the Ships Registry to see if the Dark Cloud is still on there, but there's no free internet access here; what kind of backwater is this?"

"I don't suppose it matters too much," Conner shrugged.

"Except if it's true, Nic is out of a job and might be looking for work," Ryan nodded knowingly.

"The kind of the work the Kneasleys might offer?" Conner suggested.

"Exactly."

Ryan smiled widely, "we are good!"

They spent the rest of the day in Eagle Bay, walking along both sides of the quay and taking the 'eggy Su' a good way up the river. There was no sign of the Solar Ray, nor any other trawlers. It seemed the fishing industry in this area was well and truly gone. With all their supplies eaten and the day moving into evening, the teens left the harbor and headed home. They hadn't discovered any new information, except the guesswork about Nic Pelletier and the Dark Cloud.

"So, what now?" Ryan asked Conner.

"It looks like we'll have to find the Solar Ray again and follow it, see if it stops anywhere. I can't see any other way of doing it."

"If we find it, we could attach a tracking device, use a magnet and fix it under the water line."

"Do we have a tracking device?" Dawn asked casually.

"We don't even have a magnet at the moment," Ryan smirked. "I'll look into it tonight, see if it's feasible."

"And if not, we'll have to do it the hard way," Conner said, although he didn't sound very upset.

After spending the evening with their families, the teens were up bright and early again the next morning. The full battery was quickly installed by Ryan and they were ready to go. They set off full of the enthusiasm of youth. Dawn had plotted the time of sighting and direction of the Solar Ray and estimated a possible course over the next few days.

"If we head north, we should meet them coming back south, if my calculations are correct and if they didn't stop anywhere for long, and if they're following a set course," Dawn said.

"You get anywhere with the tracker idea, Ry?" Conner asked.

"Not really. It turns out the kind of tracker in our price range is only good for about five miles, and we'd be able to see them ourselves at that distance. If we had a directional antenna, we could increase that, but that's even more money."

"Ok, everyone keep your eyes open then, that won't cost us anything."

Ryan didn't need any encouragement to use his binoculars. He was soon scanning all around looking for the ship. He had two white rings around his eyes now; he'd been using them so long.

At Dawn's suggestion, Conner headed towards Gray Island, made sure the trawler wasn't on the other side of it, then turned north. The day wore on and they saw nothing but tourist boats and container ships. They stopped at Crow Head Island again, quickly checked for traps, then had a picnic on the beach. Ryan and Terry went up to the highest point and looked around, but there was still no sign of the Solar Ray.

Later in the day, getting on towards evening, Ryan spotted something.

"There's a ship, on the horizon. Just a smudge at the moment. It looks red at the front."

Conner turned the 'eggy Su' in the direction Ryan was looking. "Tell me when you're sure, we don't want to head straight for it."

The minutes ticked by, all of them watching and waiting for Ryan to confirm the sighting.

"I see red, definitely red, it is a trawler, coming this way at cruising speed. Can't see any nets or anything deployed."

Conner turned slightly west. "I'm going to move us you can see it side on. We only need to confirm the name and we can follow it from this distance."

"Ok, one sec."

One second turned into a couple of minutes. Then, "Yep, confirmed, the Solar Ray."

"Cool, let's follow it as long as we can. If we back off enough, they won't even be able to see us."

"I can't see anyone on deck, they just look like they're out for a cruise."

Dawn was consulting her map. "If they've only just got back here, they must either have stopped or gone a lot further north, or both. They're going to be in Nova Scotia if they go much further."

"I don't think they'd risk going into Canadian waters," Conner said, "so they probably stopped for the night or maybe longer."

"Unless they're smuggling something in to or out of Canada," Terry suggested.

"Let's just add that to the whole list of possibilities we have," Jenna said.

They shadowed the Solar Ray as it headed south, losing daylight as it sailed past all the islands. The teens followed it as long as they could, and were rewarded with the sight of the trawler making a wide turn around Battle Cove Island and heading back north. The old trawler maintained the same speed and they never saw anyone on deck. They tailed it for a while as it carried on north, until they were level with Stonehaven Harbor.

"What are they doing?" Dawn asked as they turned away and headed home before it got too dark to see.

"I don't know," Conner answered. "They can't be smuggling anything because they didn't stop."

"Something illegal, I'm sure," Ryan said. "Maybe there's a mini-sub that docks underneath it, and that's how they're getting things on and off."

Dawn sighed. "Don't start with the submarines again."

"So how do you explain what they're doing?"

"By applying logic and known facts."

"Which are?"

"The Kneasleys have bought a trawler and are now sailing it up and down the coast for some reason we haven't yet worked out."

"A criminal reason."

"We have no evidence for that," Jenna insisted.

"Yet," Ryan agreed, "so let's go find some."

They pulled into the harbor and moored up with time enough to get home while it was still light, if they hurried. Dawn's phone pinged a text message alert.

"It's from Aksel. I asked him about other trawler conversions . . . Sea Fox in for minor repairs . . . asked about other ships . . . ok. Aksel says the shipyard he visited had another trawler in but all they did was paint the hull. The trawler came in with no name and went out as the Solar Ray. Says the shipyard people claim they didn't do any work inside the trawler."

"Hmm, well that's interesting." Conner nodded.

"Doesn't get us anywhere though," Jenna said. "We still can't link the Solar Ray back to the Dark Cloud, and we know they didn't change anything inside."

"Maybe they did that themselves," Ryan said.

Jenna shrugged. "It's possible, like a lot of things, but we still don't have any proof of anything."

"We have to get on that ship, it's the only way," Conner said.

"Or we could just give up," Ryan said with a straight face.

"Really?"

"No, of course not! You should see your faces!"

"Unless we've got anything else to look into, I guess we go back to following the trawler," Conner said.

With the 'eggy Su's' batteries topped up to maximum, the teens headed out again the next day, determined to find some real evidence. The calm sea conditions and their fast boat allowed them to catch up with the trawler again only a few hours later. They guessed it had stopped for the night not long after they'd left it as it wasn't very far north. They kept back as far as possible, moving around to a different position every so often. Eventually, the trawler began to slow and Conner allowed them to catch up a little.

"Well, well, this is interesting," Ryan was practically gloating.

"What?"

"I called it!"

"What?"

"That island they're slowing down for and heading in towards the harbor, what's it called?"

"Ryan, you're really getting on my nerves!" Dawn fumed.

"It's Three Hills," Conner answered.

"Yes it is, owned and occupied by our friends the Kneasleys."

"I'm going to move us closer." Conner slowed a little and turned.

"Not directly," Terry reminded him.

"No, casually."

Conner headed the boat in the general direction of the island. He knew roughly where they were in the world and recognised the island as they got closer. He moved them in far enough to get a good view of whatever happened next. They were in a small boat, low in the water and so were unlikely to be spotted. It had been their experience so far that the Kneasleys and those associated with them weren't very observant and very rarely took even the most basic precautions to avoid being seen.

The trawler was far too large for the small harbor, so it stopped several yards out and dropped anchor. A few minutes after the ship had stopped, a small boat left and crossed over to the trawler. A rope ladder was lowered, and seven people climbed off the ship and into the boat. It was low in the water but they made it back to the harbor safely, then marched onto the island. They all headed towards the house and went inside. About half an hour later, seven people returned and were taken back to the trawler.

Ryan gave a step-by step account of what was happening. "Ok, they're coming back out. I can't see if it's the same seven people, but here they go. They aren't carrying anything I can see. No life jackets, that's naughty. Climbing up, back on board, and straight below deck."

They heard the trawler's engine rev and the metallic clanking of the anchor being weighed, so it didn't need Ryan to tell that they were on the move again. They let it get a good start on them, then headed indirectly after it.

"What was that all about?" Ryan said, finally lowering the binoculars.

"Toilet break?" Conner laughed.

"There's almost certainly a toilet on the trawler," Dawn said.

Ryan shrugged, "maybe it's faulty."

"I don't think they'd be going back out to sea with broken plumbing." Dawn sighed.

"It's more likely they were reporting in to the big boss, getting their new orders or something." Conner guessed.

"Possibly," Dawn said distractedly, making notes on her phone.

For the next few hours, the trawler headed north, just like it had been before. It maintained a steady speed of a few knots. As it had also done before, the trawler sometimes went to the port side of an island, sometimes to the starboard, with no real reason the teens could see for choosing either. And still no one came up on deck nor did any kind of research. It was late afternoon when the trawler passed another island. It began to slow off shore from a wide cove, then gained speed again, as if they'd seen something suspicious.

"Where are we exactly?" Conner asked. "We're quite a way north of Rogue Island I'm guessing, not somewhere I've been before."

Dawn was checking their GPS position and looking through the charts on her phone, mumbling to herself.

"We're not that far from Canadian waters," Terry said. "We came up here in my uncle's plane once, turned around at the actual border."

"Ok, this looks like it," Dawn showed them the island in her screen. "Cape Scot Island."

"Wow, we are a long way north."

"Wait," Dawn said, her eyes wide. "I think it is the Scot Marty and tennis coach were talking about. Scot island, not Scott the name with two Ts!"

"Makes sense. And I think they're going to stop here," Conner said. "Did you see how the trawler slowed down, then took off again?"

"Like they were checking it out before actually stopping?" Ryan said.

"Yes. Look they're still heading north. We know they turn south again somewhere. If this island is a stopping place, we can get ahead of them and be ready when they come back."

"And if they don't stop?" Jenna asked.

"We'll be able to watch them from here and just carry on following them when they come back."

"If tennis coach came here before to check it out," Terry said, "what was he checking?"

"Do you think something has been left here?" Conner asked.

"It's possible."

"Ok, how long do you think we have?"

"Dawn, is there another island just north of here," Jenna asked.

Dawn looked at the charts. "Yes, Freeman's Stack. About ten nautical miles away."

"Which means they'll probably go around it and then head back, if they're going to."

"How do you know?"

"Human nature, and it's what they've done so far."

"Which gives us three to four hours before they get back," Conner said.

"Plenty of time to case the joint," Ryan grinned.

"To what?" Dawn asked.

"Search the place," Ryan replied.

"Why not just say that?"

"Because it's not as dramatic."

"We don't want drama, we want answers."

"Ok, let's take a quick trip around the island and if we spot a place to land and hide the boat, we get off and have a better look," Conner said.

"If we're fairly sure they intend to stop in that cove, we can moor up on the leeward side of the island." Terry suggested. "But make sure we're hidden in case they change their minds."

"Good idea." Conner twisted the throttle and headed closer to the island.

Cape Scot Island, when viewed from above, looked a little like a drop of water that had splashed onto a surface. It had several spurs of rock of various lengths reaching out into the sea from a roundish central mass about half a mile across. The rock that formed the island was a light gray and looked folded like fabric. Most of the island was covered in grass and low bushes, with some scattered woodland on the higher ground in the middle. They couldn't see any buildings from out at sea, nothing man-made at all. There were no jetties either, but the place looked like it was maintained, like a park, so someone must visit occasionally. There was no one around, and no other ships except the slowly fading trawler and the usual container ships in the far distance.

The teens put their plan into action, circumnavigating the whole island and then anchoring the 'eggy Su' on the leeward side of one of the shorter spurs. They pulled the boat as far ashore as they could on a rocky ledge and firmly secured it. There was plenty of flotsam here, so they covered the boat in dead brown kelp and fragments of fishing nets to disguise it and went inland.

What they'd observed from the sea was confirmed; the grass was about four inches long, lush and green, but it should have been longer in the middle of summer.

Terry looked around and sniffed the breeze. "There's something here."

CHAPTER SIX

BOARDING PARTY

FOOTLOOSE

Current usage:
The freedom to go wherever you want without encumbrance.

Original use:
A sail that was loose at the bottom edge or 'foot' of the sail.

The teens froze as Terry scanned the island, ready to run if trouble appeared.

He paused for a few seconds then grinned. "Goats, I think."

The others relaxed when they realised what he'd said.

"Now you're being dramatic," Dawn said, grabbing his hand.

"I thought that's what we wanted?"

"It's what Ryan wanted, the rest of us just want to know what's happening here."

"How did they get here?" Ryan asked, "the goats."

Now Dawn gave him a look.

"What? They could have swimmed here, there are swimming pigs in the Bahamas."

"Or maybe someone brought them on a boat," Dawn laughed.

Ryan nodded. "Yeah, makes more sense."

Terry led them towards the trees, keeping low and silent. The widely-spaced trunks of the pine trees barely qualified as a wood but they offered some cover. Terry stopped and looked around. The smell of goat was very strong here.

"I can't see anything so far," he said.

"We know they don't like to make much effort," Jenna said, "especially Marty and Nic. If there's anything here, I think it will be closer to the sea and somewhere near that cove they checked out."

"We haven't seen anything obvious, maybe it's buried," Conner said.

"But where?" Ryan asked.

"Somewhere they could find it easily," Dawn said.

"So buried somewhere close to the sea, and somewhere easy to find but hard to spot if you don't know where it is." Terry looked around and saw something. "Maybe we can ask them."

The others looked where he was pointing. A small herd of goats was standing about fifty yards away, watching them with their strange eyes.

"When you say ask them?" Dawn said.

Terry smiled. "I don't mean ask as in talk. Goats are intelligent and curious. If someone's been here the goats will have examined it. We just need to find a spot where there are a lot of goat footprints."

"Ok, you're the expert, lead on." Ryan smiled.

Terry moved towards the herd, looking down at the ground while keeping them in sight in case they decided to charge. There were eleven of them, all about as large as a big dog, with brown coats and white feet, small horns and brownish-yellow eyes. They were all watching him intently. Once he was within a dozen yards, the goats moved closer together and tensed, looking like they were going to stand their ground. Among the goat prints all over the soft mud, Terry spotted something out of place.

"Someone's been here," he said quietly. "There's a boot print over there."

"Where?" Conner asked, moving closer.

"Right under the goats, of course."

"Who's got some spare food?" Conner asked.

"Spare food, Con, what's that?" Ryan said with a puzzled frown.

"Ok, who's got some food they are willing to spare."

"Not me."

"I've got an apple," Dawn reached into her backpack and pulled it out.

The entire herd turned towards her and sniffed.

"Oh dear," she managed before the goats ran in her direction.

She quickly threw the apple so it rolled along the ground away from her. The herd followed it, bleating loudly. The small apple disappeared in a fraction of a second and the goats turned to look for more.

"Stay calm," Terry advised. "Let them come to you and don't make any sudden moves."

The entire herd gathered around Dawn, sniffing at her backpack and pushing each other out of the way to get closer. As it turned out, they were a friendly bunch and seemed to like the attention, once they realised there weren't getting any more food. While they were distracted, Terry examined the ground and found more boot prints, quite fresh but heavily obscured by goat prints.

"Someone was here," he said quietly. He followed the trail, which ran back towards the beach, then followed it the other direction, where it disappeared under the goat prints. "I think the goats have wiped out the tracks."

"Ok, let's move on, if these goats will let us."

The teens moved slowly away, the goats following them for a few yards, then losing interest. The herd spread out and returned to their grazing. Terry stopped suddenly.

"Did you hear that?"

"No." Dawn answered for them all.

"One of the goats stood on something that made a sound like a hollow thud."

"Which goat?"

"One of these." Terry moved towards a cluster of four goats, causing them to spread out further. "There, did you hear that?"

They all heard the sound this time, like one of the goats had walked over a wooden box. Tapping around with his foot, Terry soon found the spot and examined it. Buried just under the surface he discovered a sheet of ply, painted brown. He found a corner and lifted it up. It opened like a trapdoor, revealing a large space lined with stone, possibly the remains of an ancient building. Inside were several plastic boxes with tight-fitting lids and packs of beer bottles wrapped in clear plastic.

"Looks like we've found their supplies," he moved aside to the let the others see.

"Ok," Conner said, "check for anything illegal and then put it back. I think they'll be here soon wanting their beer."

"I told you we should ask the goats," Terry laughed.

They climbed down into the hollow and began moving the plastic crates around, leaving Jenna outside on watch. Most of the boxes were transparent enough to see into, revealing a wide variety of food and drink. To make sure they weren't missing anything, they opened some of them at random and examined the contents. They didn't find anything but normal, everyday food supplies. Next, they turned their attention to the floor and walls, finding nothing but damp stone and long-dead spiders. They all climbed out and put the crates back where they had been, dropped the wooded cover back into place and covered it all up. Terry made sure they hadn't left any prints of their own and they were done. Once they'd moved away, the goats headed straight over, obviously being able to smell the food they couldn't get at.

"There's nothing here but food, nothing illegal or dangerous we can see," Terry said when they'd finished looking and moved away from the inquisitive goats.

"I don't get it," Ryan said, "why hide food here when they can just stop in Eagle Bay or somewhere and buy supplies without being suspicious about it?"

"And shouldn't whatever they're smuggling be here?" Jenna said. "They haven't stopped yet, so it should be right there."

"The only thing I can think is this stuff is stolen or smuggled in to avoid import taxes or something." Conner suggested.

"That's possible," Dawn said. "Although I can't see a relatively small amount of food saving them much money, no more than a few hundred dollars each time."

"That's the Kneasleys," Ryan said. "They'll do anything for a few hundred dollars of extra profit. And they could have more than one smuggling operation."

Conner nodded. "True. And someone must have brought this stuff here. We could stake out the island and find out who. Or is that taking us away from the main investigation?"

"Yeah, that's opening a whole other can of worms," Ryan grinned.

Dawn pulled out her phone. "I'll make a note about it for possible follow up, but I agree with Ryan, it's not really relevant, more of a distraction."

"Let's finish our search of the island, there might be other stuff going on here," Conner said.

The teens carried on looking for a while longer, but didn't find anything else of interest. As time was getting on, they kept an eye to the north and soon noticed the trawler returning, the distinctive red stripe immediately giving it away. As they didn't know where it was going to stop, if it did, they were forced to wait until they were sure. They hid among the trees, watching the trawler approach. It stayed on the island's windward side, then moved in closer, slowing down.

As with many of the islands, Cape Scot had sandbanks around it which limited the trawler's mooring spots. Whoever the skipper of the trawler was knew these waters well, and the ship was soon approaching the cove and slowing to a stop, its bow pointing towards the island. There was a scraping sound as the hull touched the seabed and then stopped. The anchor dropped, landing only just below the surface, the chain dropping all around it. Conner wondered if Marty or Nic would have treated their own ships like this, running it aground and not really caring what happened.

Shouts of pleasure came from the ship and a ladder was dropped over the side. A RIB was winched after it and the crew appeared, all pushing to be the first down the ladder. Some of them were carrying chairs and other items, which they tied to another rope and lowered over the side. A few minutes later music began to play, and there was more cheering.

The teens had moved around the leeward side of the island and approached the cove using the low bushes as cover. They moved as silently as they could, although there wasn't much need with the noisy party in full swing.

"Looks like they're all getting off. Might be our chance to sneak aboard," Ryan said.

"Let's see how close we can get," Conner said. "If they all go for the supplies, we can make a run for it."

"Wouldn't it be better to sneak up on the trawler with the boat?" Jenna asked.

"We'd have to approach from seaward so the trawler hides us, and unless they leave us a convenient rope dangling over the side, we won't be able to get aboard that way," Terry replied.

"What if they don't all go?" Jenna asked.

"Then we wait for it to get dark," Ryan said.

"I don't like that idea."

"Ok, we can cause a distraction and then sneak on. There's only seven of them, that we've seen."

"Hmm, sounds better but I'm not fully convinced," Jenna said.

Terry then led the way through the low brush and approached what had now become something of a camp site. There were no tents as such, just a large cloth being used as a windbreak. A driftwood fire had been lit and a cooler full of the usual beer bottles was sitting on the edge of the water next to an orange RIB, washed by the gentle waves. An assortment of folding chairs had been arranged in a semi-circle a short distance from the fire. All of the crew had stripped down to shorts and vests and were laughing and generally relaxing. Terry crept silently back to the others to report. The teens had broken out their own rations and were eating things that didn't make a noise.

"Looks like they might be staying a while, a few hours at least. Marty and Nic are here, I didn't recognise any of the others. There's seven of them on the beach, so I think the ship is empty."

"They aren't collecting the supplies?" Dawn asked.

"Not so far."

"Maybe they don't need them yet. How long do you think they're staying if they don't need supplies?"

"Hard to say. They have a fire going, but no tents. Hours probably, but not overnight, unless they sleep on the ship or out in the open. And the rope ladder they used to climb off the trawler is fully visible from the beach."

"No way aboard then," Jenna said.

"Unless we can cause a distraction."

"But what?" Jenna said. "If we spook them, they'll just dash back aboard and take off."

"True. It will have to be something that gets their attention, but doesn't make them run." Conner said.

"Something's happening. One sec." Terry crawled closer, returning after only a few seconds.

"They're on the move, heading up the beach towards the hidden supplies. Marty has stayed behind. We could go now or if they do stay, we could wait until just before it's dark to sneak aboard," Terry suggested. "It's not the same as light but it's not fully dark either. And also, they're drinking beer, so they should be less alert."

The sun was low in the sky now, but it was by no means dark.

"We know they'll be a while, especially if they're carrying boxes. Let's go now, better than messing about when it's dark," Jenna didn't sound happy.

Conner nodded. "Yes, go now."

"Ok. Phones all the way off. No talking. I'll lead. If we're spotted or get split up, meet back here. If you have to take the boat out, just circle the island, anyone left behind make themselves visible and whoever's in the boat can come back. The password is Tolba."

They all looked at him as they processed this information.

"I told you it was more serious this time. We need to be careful and plan for failure."

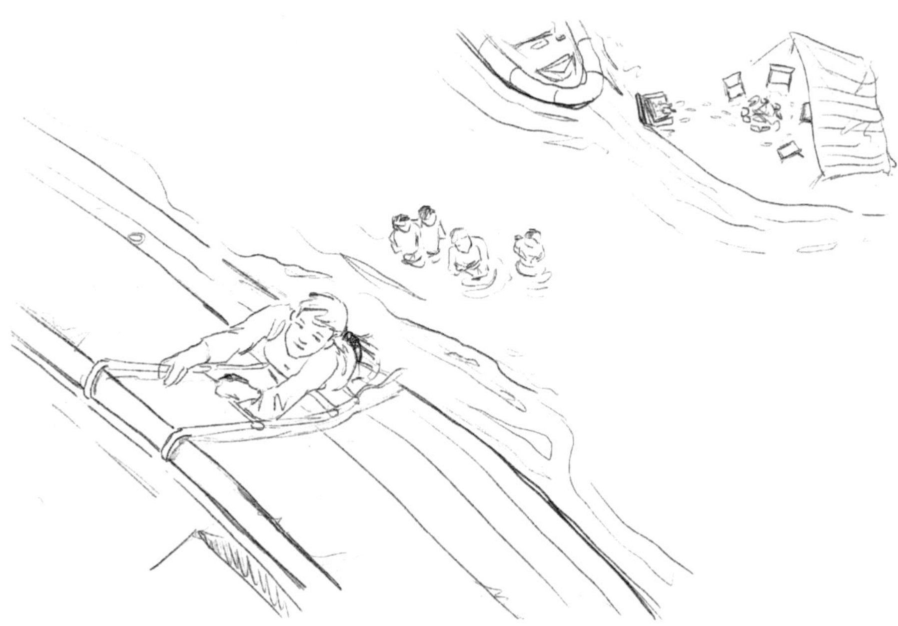

They all nodded and followed after him as he headed for the trawler. It was anchored only about twenty-five yards offshore. On land it would have been just a quick sprint, but over the sea it wasn't so easy. Terry waded up to his knees along the sandy bottom, heading for the rope they'd used to drop their camping stuff ashore, which was still hanging loose down the side of the ship. He looked along the beach at Marty. He was paying no attention to the ship at all and might even have been asleep. The boat was sitting in about ten feet of water, so Terry used his own rope and a piece of driftwood to snag the hanging rope and pull it towards him. He passed it to the others who held it taut while he climbed.

Terry's agility helped here. He was soon aboard the ship, making it seem easy. Dawn was next, and had nothing but determination to help her along. She grabbed the rope and pulled herself up, then wrapped her legs around it. Slowly but surely, she made her way up until a hand reached down and grabbed her wrist as Terry helped her aboard. Jenna went next, her upper-body strength from her swimming practice helping her quickly ascend. Ryan followed. His technique wasn't great but his natural strength got him to the top. Conner looked along the beach and realized someone was standing up. He froze, ankle deep in sea water. It was Marty, he was looking out to sea and had a walkie-talkie pressed to his ear. After a few minutes he went back to his seat and slumped down in it. Conner didn't want to be left behind, so some of the energy he put into climbing up was supplied by this thought. As he was last, the rope swung loose as he climbed and he got wetter than he would have preferred.

Once they were all gathered on the deck, and Terry had retrieved his rope, he led them over to a metal water-tight door. The teens were dripping water on the deck from their wet clothing and just had to hope no one would notice before it dried. They were familiar with this model of trawler, at least to a degree, so they were easily able to find the stairs that led down to the crew quarters. It wasn't a huge trawler, as ships go, so there wasn't much to search. There was an upper deck with the wheelhouse, a middle deck with crew bunks and the galley, and then a lower deck to store the fish. Finding the crew deck empty, Terry moved on and, mainly by smell, found the stairs down to the cargo deck.

Fading light was shining in through a porthole, revealing an open space where whatever had been down here was crudely stripped out. Of all the things they'd been expecting to find here, the teens were greatly surprised to discover a variety of old sewing machines attached to tables which were bolted to the floor. A thick cable came down through the deck above, presumably from the solar panels. A block of power cables was attached to it in a very unsafe manner. After sharing a puzzled glance, they spread out and looked around. They found some old life jackets with their seams cut open and the foam floats removed, and a small padded box which was empty. As they didn't want to touch anything, they began recording and photographing everything.

When they looked closer at the sewing machines, they found them all loaded with white thread that looked familiar. Around the machines and scattered on the floor were short lengths of nylon, the same as they'd found in the shipwreck. Dawn collected some and stashed it in her pocket for proper comparison later. There were no markings on the box at all, no labels or anything to indicate what had been inside.

Terry stopped what he was doing, then slowly moved over to one of the portholes which stood slightly open. Holding his ear to the gap, he listened for a while, then looked out and up into the sky. He waved at the others to get their attention and used his hands to mimic a plane flying in to land. They moved over to join and him and soon heard the engine noise. The plane flew over the trawler and the beach very low, then faded into the distance above the island. It repeated this motion twice more from different directions, then came in to land. It was an unmarked white sea plane, which touched down several yards off the beach, slowing but not stopping at all. The door opened, a figure leaned out, threw three small boxes into the sea, then took off again. The teens could hear Marty cursing even over the plane's engine. He was yelling at the others to launch the RIB and retrieve the packages before they sank or leaked.

Terry decided this would be a good time to leave, so he gestured for them to follow and headed for the stairs. His nose twitched as he lifted his foot and lowered it towards the first step. Very slowly he took a breath in through his nostrils. There was someone aboard. The others were very familiar with Terry by now, and knew immediately something was wrong. They froze. He turned to them, pointed upwards and gestured with one finger, then made a walking motion. As slow as molasses, he put his foot on the first step and lowered his weight onto it. When it didn't creak he moved up and did the same on the next. Once he was high enough, he peered through the gap in the open door and looked along the corridor. There was a figure standing in the shadows looking out of the door they'd entered by, presumably attracted by Marty's foul language. The figure was wearing a holster in which sat a pistol. Terry didn't know where the man had been when they sneaked aboard, but they were very lucky not to run into him. Carefully lowering himself back down, he turned to the others and shook his head. There was no way out that way.

They moved slowly over to a far corner and whispered as quietly as they could.

"Let's wait until it's dark," Terry suggested, "then sneak away when they're asleep."

The others nodded.

"Wait," Dawn hissed. "They had a cargo drop, what if they bring it down here?"

The others looked around. Apart from under the pile of life jackets, there wasn't anywhere to hide. So that's where they went. They helped bury each other until they were fairly sure they wouldn't be seen at a casual glance, then settled down to wait. The sun sank lower and the gloom turned to darkness. They heard sounds around the ship, voices, mostly Marty, shouting out orders far too loudly. Then shuffling and scraping, and finally footsteps directly above them. The voices returned, loud and obviously drunk. The music returned and grew louder as the party continued on board. Terry cautiously emerged from his hiding place, whispering for the others to stay put, although the music would have covered up an outboard engine starting.

Habit made Terry walk quietly over to the stairs. He repeated his actions of before and peeked out into the galley. There were several shapes there, including the one with the gun, who was sitting at the table with the packages in front of him. It must be something very valuable to warrant an armed guard. The man, Terry now saw under the flickering yellow lights, was smiling and singing along to the song, another one of the crew trying to persuade him to get up and dance. He didn't move and he was facing the door Terry was looking out of.

As silently as before, he returned to the others and told them about the guard, saying nothing about the pistol. It looked like it was going to be a long night as they waited for the party to run down and the crew to fall asleep. The guard would hopefully go with them, or at least go somewhere else.

The music stopped for a second, the lights flickered, and the engine started.

CHAPTER SEVEN

IN DEEP WATER

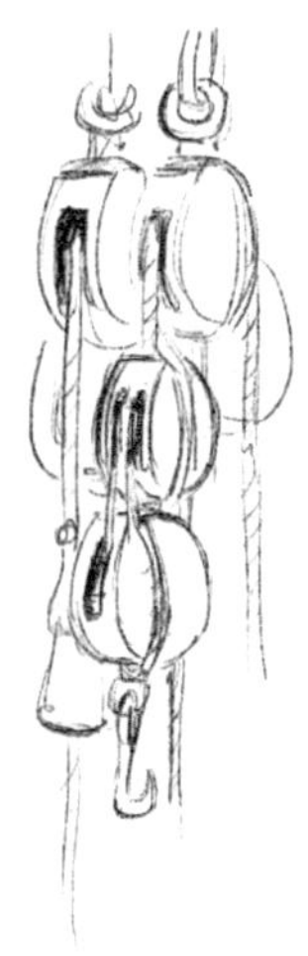

CHOCK-A-BLOCK

Current usage:
When something is completely full.

Original use:
When two reeved rope blocks came together and could not be pulled any closer.

The teens froze, hoping they were only running the generator for power, or repositioning on the current, or just turning the engine over as good practice. With the hull scraping on the sandy seabed, the ship lurched forward and the crew all cheered. It lurched again, backwards this time, then forwards, settled down and accelerated away as it turned. The teens jumped up and looked out of the portholes. They were turning south, pulling away from the island and gaining speed.

"We have to get off, now!" Dawn hissed.

"How, we can't go up the stairs, there's a guard, with a gun."

"A gun? Now you tell us," Jenna whispered.

"I didn't want to worry you."

"Ok, stay calm," Ryan said. "Let's think about this."

"The 'eggy Su' is back there, all our stuff is back there, this ship only stops twice as far as we know, here and at Three Hills, both of which are teaming with bad guys." Conner used his fingers to mark off the points. "Does that cover it?"

Ryan nodded. "Have to get off."

Terry walked over to a porthole. "This one's big enough, help me with these catches."

"Are you crazy?" Jenna said a little too loudly.

"There's no other way," Terry insisted, working at unscrewing the clamps that kept it closed. "Come on, this one won't turn."

Ryan joined him to help, while Jenna forced herself to accept the idea. She suddenly turned away and went over to the pile of foam blocks that had been removed from the life jackets. Selecting a couple of the larger ones, she stuffed them in her shirt, then a couple more to be sure. With her shirt tucked in, the blocks made a passable floatation device. She gestured for Dawn and Conner to do the same, taking some for Terry and Ryan. When they were done, they looked like robots or strangely-muscled body-builders.

The porthole finally opened with a squeak. They froze, but the music was loud up there, so they were probably ok. As they were on the lower deck the porthole was high up, only a short distance above the water line.

"Ok, lower yourself into the water," Terry said, "Don't splash. And push away from the hull as hard as you can and swim away from the wake."

They all looked at Jenna. "Ok. I'll go first then, shall I?"

Ryan made a step with his hands and Jenna climbed up and out of the Porthole. "These people owe me so many new clothes," she whispered, but didn't clarify which people she meant.

Dawn went next, then Terry and Conner. Ryan pulled himself up and struggled to get out, squeezing his wide shoulders through a gap barely big enough. He eventually made it and more fell than lowered himself into the cool, dark sea. They all swam quickly away from the dangerous propellers, leaving the trawler to sail away into the night, the party still in full swing, the crew unaware they'd even had visitors.

Unable to see anything but stars and the lights of a rapidly departing trawler, they called softly to each other, even though there was no one to overhear them. Although they could all swim, the foam floats had been a good idea. They kept the teens' heads above water without effort while they gathered together, grabbing each other in a tight circle. The cold water soon soaked them to the skin, the low waves splashing salty spray into their faces. Despite the low light in the trawler, their eyes took a while to adjust. Even then, the moonless night allowed them to see only the outlines of vague shapes.

"What now?" Dawn said, her voice shaking.

"Follow the wake back to the beach," Conner said looking around. He couldn't see it. "Can anyone see the wake, Terry?"

They all looked in what they thought was the right direction. A wave rolled in, and the glowing white foam of the wake showed momentarily in the starlight. "Over there," Conner pointed, then realised they couldn't see him. "This way."

They formed a chain with Conner in the lead. Once within the wake, it was much easier to see. Conner turned and began to swim along it, away from the distant hum of the trawler and back to the sanctuary of the island before the disturbed water settled. The current was strong, the tide going out, dragging the teens off course. For every yard they moved forwards they were pulled sideways, making them continually adjust their heading. The cold of the water was sapping their strength, and even Jenna was tiring fast.

"Not one of our better ideas," Ryan said, his voice unsteady.

"No, although the choices were limited," Conner replied.

"We could have tried for the RIB," Terry said, "climbed up the side of the ship from the porthole."

"I didn't see anything we could have used to climb," Ryan said. "No ropes or handholds."

"We shouldn't have gone in there at all," Jenna insisted. "We should have waited until it was safe to get in and out. I'm sure someone said we had to be more careful this time."

The others nodded agreement, mostly unseen in the dark.

"Let's just keep moving," Conner said, "we can blame Ryan when we get back on dry land."

"Hey!" Ryan shouted, and the others laughed. With this small boost they increased their efforts and swam towards the island, or at least where they thought it was.

Their boost of energy didn't last long, and now the wake was beginning to fade. They were bone tired, their limbs heavy and the cold penetrating deep into their bodies. They felt they'd swam twice the distance between them and safety and were still not within sight of the island.

"Wait a minute," Terry said. He listened for a while and then said, "Ok, we don't need to get back to the same beach, just to anywhere on the island. You can hear the breakers if you listen. As long as they're ahead of us we just keeping going straight."

The others listened and heard the distinctive swooshing of waves hitting the shore coming from the direction they were facing. Apart from the cold, the sound of themselves and the waves were they only things their senses registered. With their phones, PCs and TVs, they were very much part of a visual generation.

"It's not far," Conner said without really believing it. "One last push."

Staying as close together as they could and still swim, they set off once more, not fighting the current but moving with it, forwards and sideways, just like tacking in a sail boat. It felt like they were swimming through a thick shadow.

Jenna, who was slightly out in front, stopped suddenly. "Something just brushed past me."

The teens all gathered together again, each looking outwards and trying not to think about what was beneath them or just how deep the water was. It was quieter now the distant sound of the trawler had faded to nothing. They could still hear the waves hitting the island, mocking them with the suggestion of safety.

"We should keep moving, slowly." Conner said, "the waves are still breaking ahead. I think we're really close."

Reluctantly, they let go of each other and moved off, swimming using a calm breaststroke. Something broke the surface only a few feet away, disappearing before anyone could react. They tried to ignore it, keeping a steady pace towards the island they still couldn't see.

Nothing else appeared and the teens began to think whatever it was had decided to leave them alone. Then they returned; a surge of water, a light touch, the hints of lighter shapes in the dark water. First one, and then more, until the small group were surrounded. A head broke the surface right in front of Jenna, gray and with a wide smile filled with teeth.

She gasped with relief as the dolphin clicked at her, the light of the stars putting a twinkle in its eye. Others followed, more heads raised above the water and that smile that seemed to the teens as if the dolphins were laughing at these silly humans floating in the water. With more clicking and lots of head bobbing, the dolphins chatted away for a few moments, then dropped back under the water with barely a ripple. Jenna felt a nudge against her back, then an effortless force that made her surge forward through the water. The speed increased well beyond what any human swimmer could have managed. Her heart rate soared and her eyes widened with happiness and wonder. The others felt the same as they too were helped along, soon leaving the barely visible wake behind.

"Wait, do they know we want to get to the island?" Ryan said.

"It doesn't look like we have much choice," Dawn laughed nervously.

"No, this is right," Terry was smiling almost as wide as he did when looking at Dawn or playing games. "The trawler had to turn in a circle to head south, the dolphins are taking us in a straight line."

"Of course, that's clever. And this cross current is no problem for them."

"That's another reason to look after this planet, we aren't the only intelligent life here."

"Some would say we aren't even intelligent life," Ryan said.

"There's certainly evidence to support that," Conner laughed.

Each of the dolphins kept up a constant pressure on the teens' backs and after only a few short minutes, the sound of waves breaking on the shore grew louder. They'd been further out than they'd estimated. Jenna's foot hit the sea bed and she was finally able to stand. The others reached shore a few seconds after and found themselves standing waist deep in the shallows around Cape Scot Island, talking to and thanking the dolphins. Terry began to talk to them in Penobscot, his voice soft. The dolphins seemed to listen, enchanted by the rhythms. Each of the teens reached out a hand and held it palm open towards the pod. In their own time, the dolphins approached one by one, each touching the hands with their nose, lingering for a few seconds, and then turning away. The humans all stood, tears in their eyes, waiting for the dolphins to return, but they were gone. Salty tears mixed with the salty sea as the teens lingered, each deep in thought.

"Ok," said Ryan in a gruff voice, "let's get a fire going and get dry. And where's the food?"

With their eyes well adapted to the dark, the teens were able to follow the shore of the island and return to the 'eggy Su', looking out to sea occasionally hoping to catch a glimpse of the dolphins. The boat was safe and sound where they'd left it, floating on the low swell. They also retrieved the second most important thing, their food supplies.

Terry and Dawn hugged quietly for a long time, while the others sat side by side on a rock. They were wet to the skin but so deep in thought they barely noticed. Eventually, Terry and Dawn separated, and still holding hands they began to search for driftwood to make a fire.

Half an hour later they were gathered around the bright flames, drying off and toasting sandwiches as the sun rose on a new day.

"I can't believe what just happened," Conner whispered. "We were so careless, we could have been in big trouble. Then we jump off a ship into the open sea, and have the best experience of our lives."

"It was magical," Jenna sighed, "I wish I could swim with them, just for a day."

"I thought the stories of dolphins helping people were made up," Dawn said. "Now it's actually happened and people won't believe us."

"I just felt so connected to them, when I spoke to them." Terry's voice was barely audible. "It felt so natural, so right to use the language of my people."

"And you know dolphin numbers are falling all over the world," Ryan said. "We were very lucky they were around."

"One more reason people should be caring for the oceans," Conner said. "And I think I just thought of a name for the new yacht."

"The Dolphin?" Dawn asked.

"I was thinking the Smiling Dolphin, or something similar."

The others nodded in agreement; it was a suitable name.

"Do you think the dolphins would have helped us if they knew what humans are doing to the oceans?" Dawn asked, her voice low.

"Yes, I think so," Terry nodded. "They knew it was the right thing to do. And maybe they do know."

"Maybe," Dawn was thoughtful. "So, if helping us was the right thing to do, why aren't we helping them?"

"That's a very good question," Terry said.

They made camp just off the beach on Cape Scot Island. They didn't expect the trawler to return for several days, but avoided the cove in case it or someone connected to it came back. No rain was forecast so they didn't bother with the tents, just spread out in the hot sun to drive away the last of the moisture from their clothes. More food was toasted, then they let the fire burn down to embers, a faint orange glow under the bright sun. They slept for a while, leaving one person on watch. When they'd all had at least a few hours, they got back to the business at hand.

"Did it get us anywhere, that reckless action we just did?" Conner asked.

"We know what's on the trawler now," Ryan said. "Sewing machines. But what are they for?"

"I don't know. Maybe they're a red herring. The real question is what was in the packages dropped by the sea plane?"

"Something illegal obviously, and valuable if they need an armed guard." Dawn looked at Terry pointedly.

"I didn't tell you about the gun because I didn't want to worry you."

"Ok, I forgive you." Dawn went back to scrolling through the notes on her phone. "We're missing something. No one would waste money on a huge trawler to pick up something that would easily fit in a RIB."

"You're right," Jenna nodded. "And why sail the ship up and down the coast for a few days and then deliver them to Three Hills, which they sail past on the way south?"

"And a working trawler is actually suspicious at the moment. A RIB is a lot less conspicuous, there are dozens of them around here." Ryan added.

"Right, what next?" Dawn asked. "Getting aboard the trawler has just created more questions and not really answered any of them."

"Well, we know the packages are on the trawler, which will probably stop at Three Hills. So, the Kneasleys must move them from there, or the buyer must collect them from there." Conner said.

"Next stop, Three Hills!" Ryan laughed. "We might as well just camp there, it's where everything happens."

As they were all tired, they decided to stay on the island for the rest of the day. After a good night's sleep and an early breakfast, the teens headed for Rogue Island. They guessed the Solar Ray would take a full day to reach the southern-most point of its route and then another to reach Three Hills Island. Just in case it moved faster, and to stop the 'eggy Su' being spotted, they took the newly-named Smiling Dolphin and headed south. The wind was a gentle breeze blowing south along the coast. This made the journey quite slow and in sharp contrast to the 'eggy Su' which was one of the fastest boats on the coast. As they were on a stakeout, they didn't really need speed anyway.

Conner first took them in towards the coast and in range of the celltowers so the teens could send reassuring texts to parents and receive five or six in return. He then turned towards Three Hills and took an indirect course to the island, tacking expertly against the wind. He then turned around and headed south again, this time moving slightly faster with the wind. He moved closer to the island, and Ryan began to scan around with the binoculars. There was no sign of the trawler, nor the White Shark, the Kneasley's flashy speedboat.

Over the course of the next few hours, they took turns sailing the Smiling Dolphin to get some practice in. None of them were anywhere near as good as Conner, who seemed to instinctively read the wind and know what to do with the sail. It was warm today, although the sail actually provided them with a little shade if it was in the right place.

Around midday, Conner made a decision. "I'm going to head south for a while, see if we can find the trawler. If it's not even close there's no point being here."

The others agreed it was a good idea, so he set off, taking a wide course around the island to be sure they didn't miss anything. An hour later the trawler hadn't been found, so Conner sailed back to Three Hills and then on to Rogue Island when neither the trawler nor the White Shark had shown up.

They moored the Smiling Dolphin and swapped their stuff back into the 'eggy Su'. Before leaving, they went to see the Boat Prof, who had another project for them. He, Nat and Betty led them over to a large flat bottomed metal boat. Like the yacht when they first saw it, it had seen better days, although the hull at least looked solid.

"I think we should make the most of Betty's skills with metal work and convert this hull to a shuttle boat," the Boat Prof grinned. "We need a boat that can carry passengers and their belongings from the island across to Stonehaven. It needs to have at least six seats, plus a helm seat, and room for luggage. It needs to be electrically propelled of course. Nat can help you with that, if you need it, and Betty will teach you how to weld and fabricate metal, which is not the same as working in wood, as you know."

"Looking forward to working with you," Betty smiled broadly, her gold tooth glinting in the sun.

"Me too," Nat said.

As this wasn't Nat's area of expertise, he wandered off to work in the electronics workshop. The Boat Prof made sure they had everything they needed, and he too left, heading towards his office.

"Right, let's get you started," Betty said. "First, you'll need safety gear, particularly eye protection, which Im sure you already know. Metal is sharp, welding torches are hot and very bright, but as long as you follow the correct procedure, it's all perfectly safe."

They spent a few hours learning the basics of welding, practising on scraps of metal. Welding turned out to be more complicated and more difficult than it sounded. There were several methods to use, each with their own advantages and disadvantages, although the final result was the same. The metal pieces to be joined were clamped together and the metal was melted by the welding torch. Then, if the person was skilled enough, the metal flowed together and cooled to create the joint, basically creating a single piece of metal. Betty made it look easy, effortlessly producing a smooth join in various kinds of metal.

The teens all had a go, with varying degrees of success and enthusiasm. Ryan took to it straight away and was soon hooked, especially when Betty told him a properly welded joint was water tight.

"This is going to be very useful for our business, Con. We can make our own water-tight casings for the motors and batteries, and make a lot of the things we normally have to buy or scavenge."

"Cool. More profit for us." Con laughed.

"Yeah, and more upgrades for the 'eggy Su'."

They all managed to produce a joint of some kind after several tries, although they weren't all water-tight and varied in straightness. They soon ran out of metal with Ryan welding every scrap he could get his hands on.

"You all seem to be picking up the skills required pretty well," Betty said, taking off her huge gauntlets. "Especially you, Ryan, you're a natural. I think that's enough for one session. We can have another practice, then get moving in to some fabrication. If you could come up with some designs for the shuttle boat, we can move on to stage two." She smiled broadly. "Take care on your way home." They all thanked her and she walked away, heading for the academy office.

The teens left in the 'eggy Su' soon after, racing past Three Hills, which was annoyingly still unoccupied. Conner headed a little further south, didn't spot the trawler, and then turned for Stonehaven Harbor. They decided to head home after that and start again in the morning. A visit home, however brief, was always a good thing. They could catch up with their families, leaving out certain details, and show their parents they were happy, healthy and uninjured.

When they arrived near Three Hills Island the next morning, the trawler was already there. It was large enough to spot from a good distance away, so they didn't need to approach too close. Conner angled the boat so Ryan could see the harbor and report back on what was happening. As usual, there didn't seem to be any urgency about what the Kneasleys were doing. People were walking around, standing chatting, or sitting in the sun. After about half an hour, the people gathered together and a familiar small barge ferried them over to the trawler. At the same time, four other people climbed into a red speedboat, also familiar, and headed of towards the south.

"Can you see who's in the speedboat?" Conner asked.

Ryan tried to focus on the retreating boat for a few moments. "No, too far away."

"I say we go after the speedboat," Conner said, already turning it that general direction.

"Agreed," Dawn said, "I think we've got all we're going to get out of the trawler."

Keeping the loud and bright red boat in sight was relatively easy. It went due south and, as they'd expected, turned sharply and headed for the marina. Because there were other boats entering and leaving the marina, Conner was able to catch up to the speedboat without being noticed.

"I can see them now," Ryan said. "That's Marty for sure. That's Nic. I think the guy at the wheel is the tennis coach, and next to him is the guy from the Dead Man's Island adventure, the one who got lost. The old guy who was wearing a shirt and tie."

"Jeff," Dawn provided.

"That's him. Looks like he's still wearing his tie. Must be sweltering."

Their target moved over to a vacant mooring point and stopped. Conner guided the 'eggy Su' under a suitable jetty and also stopped, all eyes on Marty and his crew. The four men sat there for a while, Marty talking and gesturing with his hands. Once the talk was over, Marty climbed out of the boat, followed at one-minute intervals by the others.

"Talk about making it obvious," Terry laughed.

The marina had a full-time staff responsible for the security of the place, but they were always busy, especially in the summer. Most of the time they stayed near the more expensive boats, whose owners demanded a visible security presence. Because of this, smaller boats were mostly ignored and came and went without attention.

Walking like they were trying to walk casually, Marty, then Nic, headed over to the old chandlery and went inside. Soon after, the tennis coach joined them, and lastly Jeff, both looking really out of place. They emerged from the chandlery about fifteen minutes later and headed back to the boat, looking more relaxed.

"Here they come," Ryan warned. "No life jackets, again."

Dawn looked at him with a strange expression on her face. "What do you mean 'again'?"

"They did the same thing the other day, when they got on the trawler."

Dawn peered out from under the jetty. "They were wearing life jackets when they went in." She seemed to be talking to herself. "But they aren't now." She sat upright, almost banging her head against the wooden walkway above her. "Wow, how could we have missed that." She sighed.

"What?" Ryan asked.

"Life jackets!"

"I'm going to need a bit more than that, sis."

"We found old life jackets on the trawler with the foam removed, an empty box that probably used to have drugs in it and sewing machines. It's so obvious."

"I think I understand, but just tell us in case we missed something," Ryan said.

"So, the sea plane comes in and brings the drugs. The trawler picks them up and while it's sailing around looking like a research vessel, they cut open the life jackets, take out the foam, replace it with packets of drugs and use the sewing machines to sew them back up so they look like they haven't been tampered with. The next time they stop at Three Hills, the crew get off, take off their life jackets and get back on board and repeat the whole thing. Then someone else puts on the life jackets and delivers them here. If we keep watching we'll probably see someone go in the chandlery without one and come out wearing one, which then goes back on the trawler to be refilled. And around it goes."

"Now that's clever," Ryan nodded.

"And then what?" Conner asked.

"Well, that's our next step, we find out who comes to collect them. We can do that from here."

"Looks like we're going to be sitting under a jetty for a while then," Jenna sighed.

The red speedboat started its engines and left, taking the four men with it.

CHAPTER EIGHT

GOING UNDERGROUND

OVER A BARREL

Current usage:
Unable to proceed forward due to circumstances beyond your control.

Original use:
Sailors were tied or held down over a barrel prior to being flogged.

The teens stayed out of sight as they kept a watch on the chandlery. Only a handful of customers went in, even less came out with something they'd bought. People walked above their heads, talking loudly, boats of all sizes came and went, engines thrumming. A curious gull landed on the water a few yards away and watched them for a while. Ryan got bored.

"At least we know why the Kneasleys are spending money on that old trawler," Dawn said. She was reading through her notes in case she'd missed something.

"Yes, it's a floating workshop, secure meeting place and a great excuse to have all those life jackets," Jenna said. "I wonder if they came up with it?"

"Maybe, they're very devious, as we know."

Ryan stretched and groaned. "This is boring, let's go and check out the chandlery, some people have gone in and bought things, it won't look suspicious."

"Ok, but not all of us," Conner said. "I'll go because I know the right words for everything, and today Ryan can be my muscle. You lot can be on look out, text if anyone we know appears."

"Cool!" Ryan grinned.

Conner blipped the throttle and took the 'eggy Su' out into the sunshine. He found an empty berth, not the one the speedboat had used, and moored up. "We won't be long, keep watching," Conner said.

"Of course," Terry said.

"Be careful," Dawn advised.

It was a short walk to the old shed housing the chandlery. It looked like it had stood there for years; and the concrete wall of the marina had been built exactly and precisely up to the land it stood on. The wooden building was no larger than a double car garage, made entirely of wood with a few glass skylights and small windows, all badly in need of a clean. It had a slight but noticeable lean and was probably only still standing because it rested on the steep hill behind it. Conner went in first and looked around in wonder. It felt like he'd stepped back in time to the age of galleons and steamships. It was bigger inside than he was expecting, as if part of the shed was inside the bedrock. The store smelled of brass polish and timber and salty rope. Everywhere he looked the light reflected off shiny copper and brass surfaces. He saw old sextants and compasses, pocket watches and old maps, and many things he didn't know their name or use.

An old man was sitting on a stool opposite the door. He smiled, "Afternoon young uns; don't get many your age in here, not nowadays."

"This is a great little shop!" Conner said.

"Was, not so popular now the big un opened up the road, all shiny and bright and filled with electric doodads. Practically sail themselves, these modern boats. Where's the fun in that?" The man gestured around the shop. "Not much call for most of this stuff now, unless you're restoring an old boat or doing work for the T.V. people."

"We just restored a single-master," Conner felt obliged to say. "We just fitted the mast; we made it ourselves."

The man smiled, “good for you young uns, good for you.”

Conner looked around for something he could afford, feeling sorry for the old man. He found some small brass cleats, used for wrapping lines around to keep them in place. They did actually need some more for the yacht. They were in a box marked ‘everythin a dollor’ so he selected six that matched. He went over to pay the man, who smiled.

“We don’t got any bags, young un, just put em in your pocket.”

Conner did so, and then took another look around. “We’ll definitely be back,” he promised as they left.

“Tell your friends!” The man shouted with a laugh at their retreating backs.

“Lots of good stuff in there,” he said to Ryan as they walked back to the ’eggy Su’.

“Tell you what there wasn’t lots of,” Ryan said quietly.

“Life jackets.”

“Exactly. Not a single one.”

The two of them returned to the boat and told the others what they’d seen.

“If they aren’t in there, then where are they?” Dawn asked.

“That place is roomier than it looks, but there’s nowhere to hide anything bigger than a flare gun in there,” Ryan said.

“Smugglers!” Conner yelled, then clamped his hand over his mouth.

“What?” Dawn asked for them all.

Conner continued, whispering this time. “That shack is right up against the rock. I’ll bet there’s a smugglers’ tunnel under there.”

“Good thinking.” Dawn was already tapping away on her phone.

They all joined in, as it was an interesting topic. Like coastal towns around the world, the area had a rich history of smuggling. A wide variety of things had been smuggled into and out of Maine over many decades, right up to the present day. Usually, it was done to avoid paying some kind of tax or duty on imported goods like rum, tobacco and silk.

Although they were criminals, most of the early smugglers were just out to make some money to feed their families. Sometimes, the smugglers were organised gangs; and they were much more dangerous. The teens soon found old maps of the area, with smugglers' tunnels linking every place to every other; an underground network to rival any big-city subway. And they all led to secret coves, dozens of them, where the smugglers came ashore with their goods. The Maine coastline must have leaked like a sieve.

Most of the modern accounts had either directly disproved or cast doubt on the existence of most of the tunnels, apart from a handful of confirmed finds, now filled in or sealed with iron gates. Like many old tales, it seemed all the smugglers' stories were greatly exaggerated and romanticised, much like pirates, who in reality were thieves and murderers.

Terry stopped looking at his phone and leaned backwards to get a better view up the hill.

"I've just remembered what's up there." He pointed.

"The spa?" Dawn asked.

"Yep, the Kneasleys' new spa. I wonder if there's a tunnel from there to under the chandlery?"

"They could have built one if there wasn't, I suppose," Conner said.

"Or extended an old one," Jenna added.

"Do we think that's the final link?" Conner smiled.

"Looks like it," Dawn said. "Plane to trawler to chandlery to spa, it's all there, all carried in life jackets. Something expensive that's worth carrying in small quantities."

"So, we're saying it's some kind of fitness or diet drug, banned in the US?" Conner said. "If they're selling it in a health spa."

Jenna smiled widely. "Looks like I'm getting a free pizza!"

The others laughed.

"Looks that way."

"I'll bet the Kneasleys are charging their customers a lot of money for it as well," Ryan guessed.

"Gotta keep those profits coming in."

"And we don't need to wait for the life jackets to come out," Ryan said. "Because we have the whole trail of proof now."

"Well, if we're right. All we need to do is get into that tunnel, if it does exist," Dawn said.

"Ok, we wait until dark, or come back later, have a look in the old shack and take it from there."

"How do we get in?" Terry asked. "I don't think we should go breaking anything."

"No problem," Ryan assured them, "I saw the lock, well, I say lock, more like a latch."

"One problem," Dawn said. "If we wait until dark, our parents will think we've camped out, they'll ask questions if we go home late. So, we'll have to camp out and I'm not sleeping in the boat."

"We'll have to take the boat back to the harbor before it's dark; we don't have running lights," Conner said, "which means we'll have to walk back here. And we need to camp somewhere close to give us plenty of time to investigate if we find something."

"Unless we set up our tents on the coastal path there's no level ground anywhere around here." Ryan said.

"My house is fairly close. We can go back, camp in the garden and then come out later." Terry suggested.

"What about your parents?"

"They won't mind, the garden is huge and people often stay over in tents and RVs. It was deliberately set up that way."

Conner dropped them all off, with the camping gear, on the town beach and they walked over to the edge of town where Terry and his parents lived. Conner continued on to the harbor to moor up the 'eggy Su' and then walked along the seafront and back to Terry's house. They'd all been there before but they weren't regular visitors, except Dawn.

It was an old house, parts of it dating back to when Stonehaven was just a fishing village. Whole sections had been added on, knocked down, and then rebuilt in another architectural style. The Shays only stayed here during the summer, creating artwork inspired by the marine landscape. The studio was one large room with a wall of windows and a glass roof. It was filled with artworks of all kinds, including the wooden sculptures and canvasses created by Terry's parents. Family and friends visited during the long summer season, some of whom were also artists. There was no one camping here now, so they set up their tents at the end of the long lawn, away from the house so they didn't disturb anyone.

Before settling down, Terry gave them a quick tour and showed them some of the amazing art pieces created by his parents and their friends. He also showed them his bedroom, which was a large room in one of the extended sections. For a teenager's bedroom, it was very tidy. Each of the four walls was painted a different shade of green and the ceiling was black. The floor was polished oak boards with a collection of rugs, mostly in green. Along one wall, a huge oak desk had been placed. On top of it were several flat-screen monitors and a large PC case lit up with green and blue LEDs. On the wall behind it was a painting of a Penobscot elder riding a pony. This set the theme for the rest of the room; a mix of high-tech and First Nations. Terry seemed equally proud of all of it.

They returned to the tents and Terry told them some of his own memories of the place, and then some of its history. "Of course, the Penobscot have been coming here for centuries, long before there was a Stonehaven or even a settlement of any kind, or even a USA. My ancestors came out to the coast to catch fish and gather shellfish, which they were very fond of, apparently. My grandfather told me the shore was lined with old shells as far as you could see from the many years of people eating them."

"I've been coming here as long as I can remember. It's the only place I've been to see the ocean. I remember being really young and my dad taking me along the coast and teaching me the Penobscot words for all the animals we saw. I think that was the first time I realised I had this amazing ancestry." His voice went a bit shaky at this point, so he changed the subject and the conversation moved on as he told them about his PC and how many LEDs it had, and his plans for building another one with even more. The hours slipped away and it was soon time to make a move.

They set off for the marina just as the light was beginning to fade, walking out of town, along the coastal path, and merging onto the road that led down to it. Traffic was light, causing them to stop only a couple of times to hide in the shadows. The marina was lit up for the night by large floodlights and the lights on some of the vessels. The thumping bass of music came from several of the boats as they each tried to be the loudest. People were dancing on the decks of the larger yachts, chatting loudly on others. Summer time was party time it seemed. The teens carried on past the marina unnoticed, and past the Kneasleys' spa, which sat on the hill overlooking the southern end of the marina. Beyond this point was natural wilderness, mainly coastal scrublands with some clumps of native trees. It was lit only by the overspill from the marina lights. The teens kept to the edge of the light, using the shadows under the trees whenever they could. They doubled back across the scrubland towards the old shack once they were sure no one was watching. Keeping close to the wooden wall, Terry led them around to the door and let Ryan open it. True to his claim, a simple twisting and lifting motion with Conner's knife had the door open and they slipped inside.

CHAPTER NINE

JACK AND JEFF

SQUARED AWAY

Current usage:
When everything is organized and ready to move forward.

Original use:
When a ship headed down wind and the yards were set at approx. 90 degrees to the hull for faster sailing.

They stood quietly near the door, waiting for alarms to sound or dogs to attack, but it was all silent. They allowed themselves a single very dim phone flashlight and all looked around; it didn't take very long. The others kept out of the way to let Terry do his thing. He moved further inside, looking, listening and sniffing in every corner. About halfway along the back wall he stopped, then squatted down to examine the floor. There was no trapdoor, but along with the scratches and scuff marks of many feet, he found a deeper scrape, an arc curving away from one of the shelves. He moved his hands around in that area until he felt a cool draught.

"I think it's here," he whispered. "There's a cold breeze, and there are semi-circular marks on the floor possibly made by something swinging open, like a door."

The others joined in, feeling around and tapping likely places for hollows and secret panels. It was Ryan who eventually solved it, simply by pulling on part of a wooden wall display. The whole unit moved a few inches, leaving a dark gap through which a cool breeze was blowing. They'd soon worked it out and managed to get the secret entrance open enough to slip through. Behind it, there was a shallow niche in the rock and very narrow stone steps leading down into a dark hole. Terry listened for smugglers, then shone his flashlight down into the darkness and went down a few steps, his shoulders brushing the wall. He turned to the others and smiled. "There's a tunnel, leads up the hill, towards the spa I think, and I can hear the sea."

Moving silently, he went all the way down into the hole, moving slowly and ready to make a quick retreat. The steps led down about fifteen feet, they were rough and scooped in the center from the passage of many smugglers' boots. He stepped onto the floor of the tunnel, which was damp stone, and looked left and right. This part of the tunnel was so narrow Terry could touch both walls at the same time with his elbows. The roof was maybe six inches above his head. The floor was flat and worn in places, with two parallel lines running up the edges as if something like a cart had been regularly moved along it. It soon became obvious he had descended into the middle of a tunnel that ran up and down the hill. The steps they'd climbed down were cut into the tunnel wall. Both the walls and the ceiling still bore the marks of the chisels used to carve the tunnel through the bedrock. It must have taken many years.

There were no other lights or sounds apart from the waves in the distance. Terry sniffed the air, detecting a flowery smell among the salt and damp. He gestured the others down, Ryan making sure they could get back out. There was a latch to hold the secret door shut, but it was worn and barely held it in place.

Once they were all down, they risked more light, each taking out their phones. They stood still for a while, looking and listening. Their flashlights formed a bubble of light in the darkness, bright but small. The beams seemed to end suddenly, as if the light was being stopped by something physical, a pressure that was pushing back. Water dripped somewhere nearby, a single splash in the darkness. Everywhere they looked they saw the history of the place, every scratch and mark made by people now long gone. If they'd left a ghostly presence, the teens didn't see them.

Dawn broke the spell by saying, "look at this." She pointed to some crude lettering gouged into the wall at head height. "I think it says 'cove', and that thing underneath is an arrow pointing down hill." Despite whispering, her voice sounded quite loud.

"We should check it out, if we can get out that way it saves us risking going through the chandlery." Terry said.

"Yes, good idea," Dawn agreed, "and we can get back in if we need to."

Terry led them down in the direction the arrow was pointing. The sloping tunnel was clear but little used; the left-hand wall becoming modern concrete as they drew closer to the sound of gentle waves. When the marina had been built, they'd cut through the smugglers' tunnel, probably without noticing. Sure enough, they emerged right next to the sea, the waves lapping a good few yards into the tunnel. Terry popped his head out and found the entrance overgrown and almost impossible to see, at least in the dark. The cove itself was all but buried under the mass of the marina's structure. Once that was confirmed, they turned around and headed the other direction, up towards the spa. As they got closer, they all began to notice the smell. It was like someone had sprayed every type of perfume in the store to test them.

A short distance along they found a side tunnel. It wasn't as high as the main one but could still be walked along, although Ryan had to duck down. They decided to check it out just to be sure.

"There's some writing here," Dawn pointed to more crudely carved letters and another arrow. "I think it says 'cache'."

Ryan perked up. "Cash?"

"Cache as in store, not money."

"Oh."

The side tunnel led to a large room about ten yards square, probably a storage area for contraband. It looked like a natural cave the builders had added to and evened out. It was completely empty apart from a dried out and very dead rat. Now she was looking for them, Dawn found more markings, mostly worn out but some still legible.

"Wow, look at this. Names and dates everywhere. What's the earliest?" Dawn scanned the wall and found what she was looking for. "Here, 'Samuel H.–July 1812'! There might be earlier ones but they've worn away."

The others gathered around and looked at the writing, neat and even, probably carved with a knife.

"That was a long time ago," Ryan said unnecessarily.

"It was a different world back then," Conner said.

"Yeah, imagine no computers and no internet." Dawn added.

"No video games," Terry sighed.

"No pizzas," Ryan shook his head.

"This is history," Jenna whispered, "and it's hidden away down here."

"Well, well, look here," Dawn laughed. "'J. Allen 1843.' Any relation Conner?"

Conner moved over and examined the wall Dawn was pointing at. "Could be, our family has been in this area a long time. Doesn't mean they were a smuggler, could have been an explorer or something."

"Yeah, if you say so, Con," Ryan laughed.

Terry shushed them. "Remember where we are and what we're doing," he whispered.

They all fell silent and nodded, reminded they were on a quest. They retraced their steps and headed back towards the spa. They soon found another tunnel and began to think the smugglers' tales might have some truth to them. This one was very short, only about twenty yards, and ended in an old rock fall. Another tunnel came in from the side, which in turn led back to the main tunnel in a loop. The walls were gouged in some places, worn smooth in others. These tunnels had certainly been busy over the years.

The next side tunnel they found was on the right. It was long and straight and headed somewhere, but the teens turned back after fifty yards as time was getting on. They searched for markings on the wall but found nothing. Terry continued to lead them along the main tunnel, which began to turn as it climbed and then ended at a set of narrow stairs leading straight up. Much like the ones that led down from the chandlery, they were carved from the bedrock and surprisingly well-made. Dawn counted the steps as they ascended and estimated they'd climbed about twenty feet. At the top they found a natural cave shaped like a slightly flattened football. Like the rest of the tunnel system, the floor here had been worn smooth. A hole had been drilled through the modern-looking concrete ceiling, which was sealed off with a very new and shiny sheet of checker plate. The scent was very strong now, leaving them in no doubt they were under some part of the spa. They all grinned widely. This was the last link in the chain leading straight to the Kneasleys.

Terry carefully approached the hole and looked up. It was about a yard wide and a couple of feet above his outstretched arm. Ryan formed a step with his hands and lifted Terry until he could reach. The checker plate was warm to the touch. He put both hands against it and pushed, then tried to slide it in all directions.

"It won't move," he whispered.

Conner joined Ryan in supporting Terry and together all three of them pushed upwards. The plate didn't move at all.

"They must have a weight on top," Terry guessed.

"So how do they get in?" Ryan asked.

"Probably have a secret knock, or they just use radios," Conner said.

"We need to get in there, that's the last link," Jenna pointed out.

"Ok, we can either wait around until someone opens it, or come back with some lifting gear," Ryan said.

"We don't have enough supplies to wait," Dawn said. "I think we should come back later. We can get back in easy enough."

"And we don't really want to be down here when someone from up there opens it," Jenna pointed.

"Let's just have a think before we waste the whole night," Conner said. "What if that plate is an actual door and it's locked. We don't want to come back with the lifting gear and still not get in."

The teens stood around for a few minutes, each thinking what they could do. The entire tunnel system was empty, so it wasn't if they could improvise something.

"Ok, apart from knocking I got nothing," Ryan shrugged. "Let's just try all of us pushing together, and if that doesn't work, we call it a night."

Just like before, Ryan lifted Terry up until he could touch the checker plate, then Conner, Jenna and Dawn joined in, all four of them pushing with all their strength. A tiny sliver of light appeared at one end of the plate as it flexed upwards. No matter how much they tried it just wouldn't open any further.

"I doubt it would be flexing if it was a full trapdoor," Ryan said when they'd all got their breath back. "If we can get more lifting force, I think we can get in."

Reluctantly, the teens turned away and headed back down the tunnel, towards the cove and out onto the shoreline. They had to chop some of the undergrowth away, and they got their feet wet. It was a small price to pay to avoid going through the chandler's shack. They emerged in what was left of the cove; a space barely large enough for them all, hemmed in by rock, concrete and the open sea. They had to climb the three yards up the rock face but easily managed it with them all working together. A short while later they'd returned to Terry's and began to talk about how to get the checker plate to move.

Ryan came up with the best plan. "We can use a car jack and a length of timber. Put the jack on the floor, wedge the timber against the checker plate and lift. Nice and easy."

"Good idea. Anyone got a car jack?" Conner asked.

"We have one in the car," Terry said, "but I'll have to check my parents aren't using it. I don't want them to get a flat somewhere and not have a jack."

"And a length of timber?" Conner added.

"Loads of that around, it doesn't have to be anything special," Ryan said.

"We have to be able to carry it along the tunnel," Dawn said.

"Yes, obviously, but we're talking about a fence post, not a battering ram."

"We have some of those," Terry said. "There was a fence here before my parents planted the hedge. The old posts are in the garage. I think they're still solid."

"Perfect. Let's check they're long enough, and see about the jack, then all we need is to refill our supplies and get going." Conner said.

"It's a bit late to be going back now," Dawn said. "It's after midnight and we can't be in there when the spa opens."

"And I'm tired, we should wait until tonight." Jenna yawned to prove her point.

"Ok, let's sleep now and get ready when we wake up."

The teens all turned in after a late supper, with Terry going into the house to sleep in his own bed. Ryan was soon asleep, but the others missed the sound of the waves on the shore of their usual camping spots. Despite this, they slept late and were all invited in for breakfast when they awoke. Terry's parents were working in the studio so Terry made them all toast and fruit juice, then they went out to the garage to gather a fence post. Terry had spoken to his parents and got permission to use the car jack from their own vehicle. They didn't ask what he needed it for, just made him promise to return it before they had to go out.

The teens estimated how long the fence post needed to be by measuring it against Ryan with his arms raised. The post needed to fit between the jack and the checker plate and leave enough room for the jack to extend at least a few inches. If they could move the plate enough to get a camera inside and take some video footage, that would probably be all the evidence they needed to complete the chain of proof.

At first, they considered taking two posts as they didn't want to go back twice. In the end, they took the longest, which was over two yards long, and a small saw to trim it if they needed to. The jack was a scissor type, with a maximum opening height of just over a foot. It worked by turning a screw with a special tool, so Terry remembered to take that as well. The jack's maximum weight limit was two tons, which they guessed would be more than enough.

The day passed slowly, the teens talking and browsing on their phones for most of it. As the sun finally began to set, they set off, the jack and the tool in Ryan's bag, and Conner, Jenna and Dawn sharing duty carrying the fence post. Terry needed to be free to move around silently as he scouted ahead. It was a longer walk around to the cove and into the smugglers' tunnel, but much safer than going through the secret passage in the shack. As it was vacation season, it was once again party time at the marina, but still no one noticed them as they slipped by carrying a long post.

The tide was out this time, so they were able to climb down and enter the tunnel with dry feet. They kept their lights low and moved off, the tunnel as silent as before. The floral odor coming from the spa seemed stronger. Terry guessed the tunnel had been used today, which made them all extra cautious. As usual, Terry moved as silent as a cat as he scouted a few yards ahead. The others tried to copy his movements. Although they were quiet, they still made a little noise on the hard rock. With the side passages checked and found to be empty, the teens continued on to the cave under the spa. This too was silent, the checker plate still in place.

They quickly set up the car jack and the fence post and found they'd underestimated the distance. The jack was extended almost to its limit before putting any pressure on the plate. They tried it anyway, and were rewarded with a small amount of lift. Light spilled in around the gap, and the floral scent grew even stronger. Once again, Terry was lifted up by Ryan and Conner. The gap they'd made was less than two inches. He peered through and saw a wooden floor and some large boxes. This was certainly someone's basement, but there was nothing, apart from the smell, to prove it was the spa. Terry was lowered down and they moved away from the hole a little, gathering in a tight circle.

"It's a storeroom of some kind, probably the spa, but I can't be 100% certain." Terry whispered. "The good news is it's just a sheet of checker plate, no locks or hinges, probably just something heavy on top.

"But we still need to lift it higher, or slide it." Conner said.

"We could get one of those rocks from the rock fall," Ryan suggested "We could get a few more inches at least if we put one under the jack."

"Doesn't sound safe," Jenna said.

"I'm sure I saw a flat one, that'll be ok."

"Ok, you go and look, we'll let the jack down," Conner said.

Ryan and Jenna went back to the side tunnel while the others lowered the jack and removed the post. After a seemingly long wait, Ryan and Jenna returned with a heavy rock, both of them straining with the weight.

"Couldn't find a bigger rock?" Conner grinned.

"You wanted flat, this is the best we could find."

The pair dropped the rock under the hole with a deep thud. Everyone froze and listened for a reaction from above. Silence. The rock was more sort of flat than actually flat. By moving the jack around, they found the most stable place to put it. With the post in place, and everyone but Terry standing back, they lifted the plate again, this time creating a useful opening.

Ryan stood under the hole and made a step with his hands. Terry stepped up and looked through the gap, straight into someone's eyes.

"Marty, I know it's you, I'm not asleep, ok?"

Terry jumped down and grabbed the jack tool, twisting it furiously to lower the plate.

The others, who had frozen when they heard the voice, leapt into action to catch the post as it loosened. The checker plate clanged down and the voice above became a muffled shout. They heard something scraping across the plate and then it began to slide. Ryan and Jenna grabbed the post, Conner picked up the jack and Dawn grabbed the jack tool. Without a word, they dashed out of the cave, down the steps and headed back along the tunnel, just as a voice called out above them.

"Marty! It's not funny anymore. Marty?"

A bright beam of light flashed across the tunnel walls and then faded as they turned a corner. Terry led them down the main tunnel, then into the side tunnel that looped around.

"I've got a plan," he whispered.

At the end of the looped tunnel, they all stopped and listened. They heard a scraping sound, a dull thud and lots of bad language.

Terry leaned towards the others and whispered. "I think it's Jeff."

"The guy who got lost on Dead Man's Island," Ryan said.

"Yes," Terry grinned. Jeff was even worse than Marty when it came to spacial awareness.

CHAPTER TEN
UNHEALTHY SPA

TOE THE LINE

Current usage:
Follow the rules, laws and regulations or path as ordered by a superior.

Original use:
When the crew fell in line on deck for inspection or when addressed by a senior officer, the sailors lined their toes up with seams of the deck planks.

A bright light flickered along the tunnel as Jeff walked nervously along it. He glanced down the side tunnel as he passed the entrance carrying the biggest flashlight any of them had ever seen. It was more like a spotlight from a truck than anything. The light passed them by and appeared a short time later at the second entrance to the loop.

Terry gestured for them to move and he headed back towards the cave with the hole in the roof, stuffing the jack in Ryan's backpack but leaving the post behind. He headed over to the now open hole and looked up. Above them was a small storage room with white boxes stacked against the back wall. The checker plate had been slid open, leaving a hole easily large enough for them to get through. Ryan moved over and took up position and Terry climbed up him and pulled himself into the room.

"What are you doing?" Jenna hissed. "Jeff could come back any time and catch us."

"Best be quick then," Ryan whispered.

Conner went next, then Dawn, who Ryan lifted almost into the room, where Conner and Terry caught her.

Jenna hesitated. "You're crazy, all of you. What if we get caught? This is trespassing."

"We need to find the link, remember?" Ryan gestured with his hands. "Come on."

Grumbling under her breath, Jenna stepped on Ryan's hands and shoulders and easily climbed up. Terry and Conner then leaned down and caught Ryan's wrists as he jumped up from the rock and got a grip on the edge of the hole. He was the largest and heaviest of them all, but also the strongest and he was soon inside with the rest of them. There was no sign of Jeff or the huge light, so they assumed he'd gone all the way to the shack.

The room they were in was about four yards square, with the white cardboard boxes stacked almost to the ceiling on the back wall. On the opposite wall was an internal door, with a bolt on the inside, which seemed strange. The boxes were, according to the label, paper towels. Terry lifted one up and it was very light. A small but bright light-strip was positioned directly above the hole. Also in the room was a large chair with stained red padded upholstery. Two of its legs were on the checker plate. Against the side wall was a backpack and a large red Thermos.

Terry smiled. "Looks like it was Jeff blocking the hole, and he must have been asleep the first time we moved the plate."

"Wait 'til Marty finds out!" Conner laughed.

Terry moved over to the door and eased open the bolt. It looked new and so slid quietly. He listened for a moment, didn't hear anything, and slowly opened the door a fraction of an inch. Beyond was a corridor in darkness, the door at the end of it. There was light coming from somewhere beyond the corridor. The floral smell was so strong it had become more of a taste now.

With no sight or sound of Jeff, Terry led them out into the corridor and scouted ahead. Dawn was now recording everything while Conner took still pictures. Ryan was shadowing Terry in case something went wrong. Jenna was at the rear. She wasn't mumbling now, but she was still thinking how stupid they were being and how she was doubly stupid for following them.

The teens had no trouble moving silently along the thickly-carpeted hallway. They turned left at the end and emerged onto a wide balcony surrounding an oval pool with several smaller pools and hot tubs around it. On the opposite side to them was a large seating area and a small café overlooking the marina and the sea. Almost everywhere they looked there was tinted glass.

The light they'd seen was coming from an office overlooking the sea. It was basically a glass box with a large desk and several chairs inside. Despite the late hour, a meeting was taking place within. They could clearly see Renzo and Regina Kneasley sitting on one side of the large desk. To one side, and looking very bored, were Marty and the bald man from the speedboat, possibly called Seb. On the other side of the desk, their backs to the teens, sat two other figures. They were both wearing dark clothing and had shoulder length black hair. On the table between them were several small bottles and some larger ones.

One of the figures leaned forward and opened a larger bottle, mostly filled with a clear liquid, and poured the contents of a small bottle into it. The person then shook the bottle and held it up. The Kneasleys smiled and nodded. The conversation continued for a while, with a lot of smiles and gestures to the bottles. They all suddenly stopped and looked at Marty, the Kneasleys looked very annoyed.

Marty sheepishly pulled out his phone, and then looked up, out into the spa.

"I think Jeff just realised it wasn't Marty down there," Terry whispered. "Come on, let's get out."

Terry turned them around and Jenna led the way back to the storeroom. Following Terry's example, she slowly and carefully opened the door a little, then immediately closed it.

"There's a huge beam of light in the hole," she explained. "Jeff's found his way back."

"Let's go, look for a fire door." Terry headed off at some speed, deeper into the spa.

When they reached the end of the corridor, Marty and the speedboat man were in the office doorway, arguing with Renzo. He was shouting something about poor security, while Regina was calming the two strangers.

Terry led them along the darkened edge of the balcony and towards another corridor that ran down the side of the spa. Once they were out of sight, and with Marty and speedboat man now on the move, Terry led them to the end of the corridor where a dull emergency light sat illuminating a sign that said 'Fire Exit'.

They quickly made their way over to it and soon discovered it was locked with a stout chain and a large padlock.

"I'm sure that's illegal," Dawn whispered.

"I don't really think they care," Terry answered.

They moved over to one of the side doors, hoping to find a window to climb out of. The sign on the door read 'Treatment Room F' and when they looked inside it was a small room with a massage table and a wall rack with fancy bottles on it.

"Nowhere to hide in there, try the next one," Terry suggested.

They checked all the treatment rooms up to A and found a similar set up in them all. They tried the other side of the corridor, while voices shouted back and forth, some of them very close. More doors were tried until, with someone just around the corner, they found one marked 'Roof–Staff Only'

They slipped inside just as a shadow fell across the corridor. Ryan gestured to the others and then gripped the door handle and put his weight against the door. The others copied, then waited in silence. Someone moved around outside. They heard a door swing open, then another. It all went quiet, then suddenly the door moved. They held on with all their strength as whoever it was pushed against it. The person mumbled something, then moved off. Another door squeaked open and after a few moments of silence someone said, "there's no one here, old Jeff must have been dreaming.

"Yeah yeah, I'll keep looking."

The teens moved away from the door when silence fell.

"Right, it's not likely they'll search here again, at least for a while," Terry said.

"I've got a plan," Dawn said. "The spa is built into the hill, so if we can get onto the roof we just drop down at the back and escape that way."

"It will still be a high drop," Jenna said.

"It's worth a look, at least," Conner said.

They all agreed they had no other safe way out so they would give it a try. The stairs went up and around, delivering them to a short landing. At the end was the exit onto the roof. It wasn't a fire exit, but it was firmly locked. A barred gate was held shut by a stout padlock and beyond that was a locked exterior door.

"Ok, let's not go that way then," Conner said.

The teens all went back down the stairs. Terry listened at the door, then opened it a fraction. The darkened corridor was silent, although he could hear voices some distance away.

"It's clear, but what now?"

"Let's see if we can make it to the front door, the Kneasleys must have come in somewhere, maybe they didn't lock it," Conner said.

"It's a big risk," Jenna pointed out. "If they see us, we have nowhere to run."

Conner shrugged, "I'm really running out of ideas here."

"It's pretty dark out there, do what I do and don't make a sound," Terry opened the door a little and prepared to move.

"I know it's dark, but everything in here is made of glass," Jenna said nervously.

"It's fine. Stay low, move slow. People see what they want to see," Terry said wisely.

The others nodded but didn't speak. Terry opened the door enough to slip out and moved away to let the others out. He made his way to the end of the corridor and peered around the corner. He could see the office and Regina sitting inside reading something on the desk. There was no sign of anyone else. He would have preferred to know where they'd gone, but if they weren't here it would have to do. The stairs to the balcony were at the end next to a small elevator. The stairs, and indeed the elevator, were panelled in glass. They led down to an open area near the pool, where a long decorative plant arrangement partially screened off the main pool. It would make an ideal place to hide as they moved towards the main doors, as long as no one was down there. He turned to the others and raised his eyebrows in question. They all nodded they were ready and he stepped out of the corridor.

The lights came on.

The others turned and ran back. Terry moved slowly back into cover and then into the stairwell they'd just left.

"What now?" Ryan asked almost casually.

"We've done it again," Conner said angrily. "We've got ourselves stuck because we weren't thinking."

"Let's think now," Dawn said. "We aren't caught yet."

"I don't think anyone saw us, but we can't go walking around out there now," Terry said.

"Ok, the only way out is the roof, so how do we go about solving that problem?" Dawn asked as if she already had the answer.

"We can't get out of a locked door, never mind an iron gate," Conner said a little too loudly.

"We've still got the jack," Ryan pointed out.

They all looked at him, and then ran up the stairs to give it a try.

"Right, we have one jack and two doors. What now?"

Dawn smiled. "It's just one of those logic problems. You know, like crossing the river with the fox and the chicken and the bag of corn."

They looked at her blankly.

"Never mind. Look, the jack only opens and closes, so that's what we have to do."

"And fast," Terry pointed out.

"Right. We put the jack between the gate and the door and open it out to push open the door, then we use the jack to push the bars apart and climb through."

"What about the noise?" Jenna said.

"Oh, the waterfall in the pool came on with the lights, should be plenty of noise," Terry said.

They flattened the jack as far as it would go, then jammed it in the gap between the outer door and the gate. When it was opened it pushed against the door, but then the gate started to bulge outwards.

"That's no good, Ryan said. "If the gate opens, we won't be able to put pressure on the door."

"Brace it," Conner said.

They all leaned their body weight against the door while Dawn, the lightest, turned the jack tool. Both doors began to bow until the top of the jack made a hole in the door without pushing it open. They repositioned the jack and tried again, aware that time was slipping away. They were all sweating by the time the outer door burst open with a crack and the pinging of metal.

An alarm activated, blaring out all over the spa.

Beyond the door they could see the roof, but the gate was still closed. Working quickly, aware they only had a few seconds, they pushed the jack between two of the bars and frantically twisted the jack tool. It seemed to take forever to even engage with the metal, then push the bars wider apart.

"Damn! we've done it wrong. Move the jack down, we need to break the weld and take the bar out, we'll never get through there!" Ryan retracted the jack until it slid down to the centre brace of the door where the bars were all welded in place. He wound it out again and kept going until the weld failed and the bottom of the whole bar was loose. He grabbed and bent it outwards, the others joining in as he struggled with it.

They heard voices approaching, someone shouted. "I don't know, I've never been in this part."

Dawn went through the gap then turned to help Conner. Jenna went next, then Ryan. The door at the bottom of the stairs opened and the same voice said, "ok, I've found it. Yeah, I know!"

Conner ran over to the edge of the roof and looked down. It was still dark, but enough of the light from the marina and its surroundings let him see the hillside was quite close to the roof, but not that close.

Ryan helped Terry through, who then stopped to retrieve the jack.

"Leave it!" Ryan hissed as he heard footsteps on the stairs.

Terry shook his head, frantically winding the jack tool until the jack came free. He grabbed it and turned to run towards the others, who here hiding behind an A/C unit. He signalled to Ryan to turn around and he stuffed the jack and tool into his backpack, then assessed the situation.

"How far down?" he whispered.

"About fifteen feet," Conner said.

"Hmm, bit too high. We need a rope." He reached into his pocket and pulled out a length of mooring line about twelve feet long. "Better than nothing."

They heard the man on the stairs. "What the..? Any bears around here? This roof door's been ripped open."

There were a few moments of silence and the man replied. "I'm not going out there, I don't care what you say. If you're so brave, do it yourself."

The man disappeared back inside, still arguing.

Terry moved over to the edge and found the lowest part of the roof. He then tied the rope to the closest anchor point, which was one of the pipes running to the A/C unit. The knot shortened the amount of rope they could use to descend; it would have to do. Jenna went first. She was the most agile and tall enough to reach the floor if she let herself down as far as the rope would go. Ryan went next, then Dawn, who had to be helped as she couldn't quite reach the ground. Then Conner.

Terry hesitated as Conner went over the edge. "What about the rope?"

"What about it?" Conner grunted as he stopped himself.

"Well, it points to us."

"That can't be helped, get down here."

Terry nodded. But when Conner reached the bottom, the rope disappeared.

Dawn gasped. "What's he doing?"

The rope reappeared, this time considerably shorter. He climbed down it as far as he could, which still left him a good ten feet above the floor.

"Ready?" he hissed.

"What?"

"Catch me."

"Are you crazy?"

Conner now realised Terry had looped the rope around the pipe and was holding the two loose ends, one in each hand. When they'd gathered beneath him, he let go with one hand. Instead of plummeting to the ground he was lowered at a leisurely pace and only dropped a few feet, the rope falling down on top of him. He grinned in triumph.

"How did you do that?" Ryan asked

"Why did you do that?" Dawn demanded, giving him a hug.

"The pipe was smooth. I just wrapped the rope around a few times and when I let go it slid around. And now I have the rope and they won't know where we went."

Voices sounded above and the teens melted into the undergrowth.

"It's not a bear!" Marty yelled. "How does a bear get on a roof in the middle of town?"

The other person, probably speedboat man, answered. "I don't know and I don't care. What else can rip a door open like that? I've seen videos on the internet. They just put their claws in the tiny gaps around a car door and take the whole thing off. Wham!"

"Why would a bear break into a health spa?"

"I don't know. Maybe it wanted a massage."

There was a moment of silence, then Marty and speedboat man burst out laughing. In the foliage below, the teens had to cover their mouths before they did the same.

"Doesn't answer the other question," Marty said. "If someone's inside, where did they go?"

"Maybe the bear got them."

"You're such an idiot."

"Yeah, but at least I wasn't asleep on the job."

The teens waited silently until the voices had faded and then made their way down the hillside. It was steeper than they had thought and only the plentiful bushes and trees giving them handholds let them descend at all. They were as quiet as they could manage. Now they were on public land they weren't breaking any laws, but five teens climbing down a hill in the dark did look suspicious. As they approached the side of the building Terry froze. The others did the same a few seconds after. They looked around to see what he was reacting to, and heard voices. In the quiet of the night, they were clearly audible, coming from somewhere near the side entrance to the spa. One of the voices was Renzo, the other possibly one of the strangers.

". . . can assure you everything is under control. We've searched everywhere and it was a false alarm. My security team have everything under control."

Someone spoke in what sounded like a Slavic language, the other then, presumably, translated in a thick Slavic accent. "My associate is not happy. Not believe you have bear."

The first man spoke again, a long sentence, but the second man only said. "As you Americans say, 'get grip'."

"Everything is fine, we'll search all night if we must, but I'm convinced it was faulty wiring. There are no problems here, we'll get rid of the weak link in our security, and there are definitely no bears." Renzo sounded very worried.

The first man spoke again, then they walked off without explanation. The teens watched them go but weren't able to see what vehicle they got into. Renzo stayed outside for a while, then went in the staff entrance and firmly locked the door.

"What was that about?" Ryan said.

"I'll tell you when I've translated this recording." Dawn tapped her phone screen then put it away.

Ryan tried not to be impressed. "Yeah, obviously."

CHAPTER ELEVEN

THE FINAL VOYAGE

MAINSTAY

Current usage:
The main item or point to support a proposal or action.

Original use:
The first piece of standing rigging placed after the mainmast is set in place. The mainstay helped to support all the rigging that followed and was essential to keeping the lower mainmast upright.

The teens waited a while longer to make sure no one would return, then they crept down the hill to the marina and headed back to Terry's, keeping out of sight as much as they could. The jack and the jack tool were safely returned to his parents' car. The fence post was lost but easily replaceable, should it be needed in the future. It was only a few hours until sunrise, so the teens all turned in and tried to sleep.

Later that day, bleary-eyed and barely awake, they gathered in Terry's kitchen for breakfast and to discuss the events in the spa. Talk centered mainly around what they were calling the Russians, two new characters in this adventure. Dawn was playing the recording of the conversation in the parking lot into her earphones and translating it via an app on the internet.

After several minutes she pulled out the earphones and looked around the table to make sure they were all listening, particularly Ryan. "I think I've got it right. I'm fairly certain it was Russian. This is what I have, edited for a family audience.

"Renzo says '. . . it was a false alarm . . .' the first guy speaks without the second guy translating, 'They are all a bunch of bleeping morons, why would they make up a bleeping story about a bear? Why are we wasting our time with these clowns?'

"The second guy then translates that as 'my associate is not happy. Not believe you have bear.'

"Then the first guy speaks again, 'they are going to ruin everything. This is a sweet operation and these bleeping clowns are going to bleep it away down the bleeping drain. Tell them to get it fixed, I'm going home.'

"The second guy says 'as you Americans say, 'get grip'.

"Renzo says 'everything is fine, etc.'

"Then the first guy says 'we'll be rid of them in a few days, then our people can take over.'

"That last part is a little concerning. What do you think they meant?"

"It either means the Kneasleys are going to be unemployed or disappeared," Ryan said bluntly.

"If their lives are in danger, we have to warn them," Jenna said.

"Why would we help the Kneasleys?" Ryan asked sharply, "after all they've done."

"Because it's the right thing to do."

"Besides," Conner pointed out, "they can't go to jail if they disappear."

Ryan calmed "True, I suppose."

"We could just send them the recording and say 'translate this'," Terry suggested.

"Yes, and leave it up to them what they do next," Ryan replied.

"Ok." Dawn began tapping away on her phone, "they both have email addresses on the ReKnew website, I'll send it to both and mark it urgent."

"Won't they know who sent it?" Jenna asked.

"No, I have an anonymous email address."

"You do?"

"Of course, how do you think I've been sending things to the police?"

"Oh, ok."

"How do we know they got the message," Jenna asked. "What if they don't check, or the emails get spam filtered?"

Conner reached over and patted her arm. "We can go to Three Hills and see what's happening, if you want?"

"Yes, I think it would be worth checking out."

"We can go on the way to the academy, and on the way back, it's not too far out of the way."

"Ok. So, who wants pizza for lunch?"

They all did, of course, and after lunch at Conner's parents' pizzeria, they went down to the harbor and took the 'eggy Su' out just because they'd been away for two days. Conner subconsciously took them towards Three Hills Island. The Kneasleys' boat was in the harbor; but there was no sign of them or anyone else, no suitcases piled on the quay or signs of frantic packing. They would just have to trust the Kneasleys had got the message and were doing something about it other than getting out of there.

"The Russian said a 'few days, right?" Conner asked Dawn.

"Yes, which is maybe three days at the most. They need to get a move on."

"It's only been a few hours since you sent the emails, they probably haven't seen them yet." Ryan said.

"Yeah, you know what these old people are like," Terry grinned, "they only check once or twice a day."

Jenna sighed, "well that's not going to turn out well for them. They need to get moving."

"Apart from knocking on their door and telling them to check their emails, I don't see what else we can do" Ryan said.

"Perhaps we should have sent the recording to the police," Conner said, "then they could arrest the Kneasleys while saving their lives."

"Well, we still can," Dawn pointed out.

"I'm not really sure why we didn't anyway," Jenna said.

"There's not much to go on for the police, and they would have had to investigate, which would take time." Terry said. "The Kneasleys will know straight away what's going on."

Conner turned the boat away from the island and headed back to the harbor. "I'll take us ashore. As soon as you're in range, Dawn, send the email to the PD."

"OK, let me get it ready."

"Too late," Terry said quietly. "Ryan, check out this boat."

Ryan grabbed his binoculars and looked where Terry was pointing. A small and quite tatty black boat was approaching Three Hills Island from the south. It had straight sides and a boxy look; It was probably a river boat. Luckily for the occupants the sea was calm today. It had a small motor that was being revved hard, and it had only two seats, both occupied by men with dark clothing and shoulder-length black hair.

"It looks like them, the Russians from the spa," Ryan said.

The boat headed for the harbor and one of the men jumped out and moored the boat next to the Kneasleys' speedboat. The second man climbed out and they both headed towards the house, seemingly not paying any attention to anything other than where they were going.

"Move closer, right in if you can, but keep hidden." Terry said. "Find somewhere we can see the harbor and the house, but not be seen ourselves."

"That's not going to be easy," Conner mumbled.

"Try those trees next to the big rock."

Conner moved in closer, blipping the throttle then drifting for maximum stealth. They soon found a spot they could hide and still see the harbor, but not the house. Terry leapt ashore, moved over to a tree and climbed a little way up into the branches. He turned and gave the others a thumbs up, then turned his attention to the house.

"What if those Russians are armed, they might already be murdering the Kneasleys," Jenna said.

"There's nothing we can do if they are," Ryan said, "we'll just put ourselves in danger."

"What about using a flare to call in the Coast Guard?" Dawn suggested.

"No, not yet." Conner answered. "If they're just in there talking, we could get in trouble and alert the Russians to what we're doing."

They settled down to wait, something they were well-practiced in after all their adventures. A few moments later, Dawn realised she couldn't see Terry any more.

"Where's Terry?" She asked, her voice a little shaky.

They all looked up into the tree he'd been occupying. There was no sign of him there or anywhere else.

"I think he's gone over to the house," Conner said.

"On his own? Why would he do that? Move closer, I'm going in."

"Dawn, he'll be fine," Conner reassured her. "We can move in and wait for him, but we need to be ready to move."

"I'm going ashore, not too far. I'll come straight back when I see him." Dawn was already climbing out of the boat at this point.

"Stay low, and be quiet," Ryan advised.

She gave him a look. "I've been with Terry for over a year, I've learned a few things."

With that, she ran up the slope and disappeared among the trees.

Jenna nodded. "She's right, can't see her at all."

Ryan didn't speak; he was obviously worried.

Terry watched the two men approach the house. He was surprised when one of them actually rang the doorbell. A short time later, Regina appeared and smiled, before standing aside and letting them in. So, he thought, they hadn't checked their emails. Once the door was closed, he moved closer, using the newly-planted hedges of the formal garden to get closer. There were no cameras he could see, except maybe on the doorbell, and no sight or sound of any dogs. If I lived out here miles from the shore, he thought, I'd have dogs, and cameras, and open my emails.

Keeping to the shaded part of the house, he moved over to the nearest window and cautiously looked inside. He found a large study, painted almost entirely white and with the absolute minimum of furniture. There was no one here, but he could hear voices, slightly raised but not shouting. He moved a little so he could look out of the door and into another part of the house. He saw a shadow moving but no people. Now he knew approximately where they were, Terry moved around to what he thought was the correct window and crouched beneath it, just out of sight. Inside, there was a conversation taking place, a little one-sided, as the Russian who spoke English asked the Kneasleys a constant series of questions. Terry tried to listen, but the words were muffled by the triple-glazed windows.

As the situation escalated and both sides got louder, the words grew clearer. It soon became obvious the Russian wasn't getting acceptable answers to his questions, as both of the men were getting angry. Renzo was trying to calm them down.

"Who knows? Tell me!"

"Look, if you'll just calm down, we can sort this out."

There was some shouting in Russian, then more in English. "We will sort this out when we have answers. Is it one of your men, or someone outside?"

"I have no idea what you're . . ." There was a slapping sound and several bumps.

Regina yelled, "leave him alone!"

The Russians ignored her. "Where is your safe! Let's see what secrets you have."

"Please, I don't have a safe, there's nothing to hide, I can assure you . . ."

Another slap, then furniture scraping along the floor.

"If you want to still be married in future you should tell us the truth."

"Renzo, just give them what they want. I told you we're in too deep."

"Fine. But there's not much to see."

The noise faded and Terry risked a glance inside. The two men and the Kneasleys had moved into another room. Terry sneaked around until he was under another window. This one was in shadow and an evergreen tree had been planted beside it. Using the foliage to hide behind, he peered into the room. This study was made of wood. Everything from floor to ceiling, including the walls, was polished wood. Renzo had gone over to a cupboard and opened it, and was reaching inside. He stepped back after a few moments and the Russian took over. He had soon dragged out a pile of documents and a large stack of money, which he gave to the other man.

The two looked through the stack, one translating for the other. At some point, their anger turned to smiles, they removed some of the papers and threw the rest back into the cupboard.

"Good, we have what we need. Now, we will go for a small trip on boat."

Renzo made a dash for the door. He was very slow and clumsy and was never going to make it. Sure enough, the Russian who didn't speak English punched him in the side of the head and he collapsed in a heap.

The two men laughed and exchanged a few words in Russian. Dawn is going to be mad at me for not recording this, he thought. With the documents in his pocket, the man pulled a now bloody Renzo to his feet and dragged him out of the door. The other did the same with Regina. None of them spoke as they made their way to the front door.

Terry moved around so he would see them when they came out. There was a short delay, then they emerged. One of the Russians came out first and headed for the harbor. Renzo and Regina came next, their hands secured behind their backs with zip ties. The second Russian came out next, leaving the door wide open.

Terry moved around into the remaining natural undergrowth and ghosted around towards where the 'eggy Su' was moored. He caught a faint odour of perfume and smiled. There wasn't really time to tease Dawn, so he moved straight towards her hiding place. To her credit, she had turned towards him as he arrived; he hadn't completely taken her by surprise. They exchanged a glance and then dashed back to the boat.

The small group appeared at the harbor, the Kneasleys walking slowly with their heads down. Renzo's shirt collar was now red with blood. Both of the dark-haired men had their right hand inside their thin jacket. First Regina and then Renzo were ordered into their boat, the White Shark, which wasn't easy with tied hands. They eventually managed to stumble into the back seats. One of the Russians climbed into the front and started the large engines with a roar. The other man returned to the black boat, started the boat's tiny engine and then waited as the other man reversed out of the harbor and turned towards the open sea.

Terry and Dawn returned, leaping into the 'eggy Su' and taking their usual positions. Conner edged them around the large rock until they could peer around it and see what the Russians were doing. The two boats had stopped at the side of the island. The White shark was pointing east towards the open sea. Conner had a sudden feeling he knew what was about to happen. Sure enough, the man in the White Shark clambered over to the other boat, leaned back into the Kneasleys boat, then turned to them and said something. With a wide grin and a mock salute, he pushed the White Shark's throttle fully forward and pulled back as the engines revved. The boat gathered speed before shooting away. The two men watched the boat as it headed out to sea in a relatively straight line. One of them waved and said something, the other laughed loudly. The small boat then turned and headed south in no particular rush.

They couldn't just race after the Kneasleys in case the Russians looked back and saw them. There was no way their tiny engine could catch them, but it looked like they had guns and they might have had help waiting somewhere. Conner turned the 'eggy Su' around and headed for the north side of the island where they couldn't be seen. He then turned east, twisted the throttle as far as it would go and set off in pursuit of the runaway boat.

"Can we catch them?" Jenna asked.

"This is the fastest boat on the whole coast, if we can't they're in big trouble," Ryan said.

"Should we use a flare?" Dawn asked.

"The Russians will see it."

"Does it matter now?"

Conner shrugged, "I suppose not. I doubt they'll come back and risk the Coast Guard turning up."

Dawn opened the locker under the rear thwart and pulled a flare out of its waterproof package. They'd all trained in their use, so Dawn wasted no time in setting it off. There was a whoosh and a few seconds later a loud crack. A bright red fire appeared above them and streaked upwards before slowly falling back down. Anyone within a huge area would see it and know someone needed aid and where to find them.

The wake from the White Shark's large engines was easy to follow; as if the roar of those engines wasn't enough. Conner had the throttle fully open now, the electric motor humming like a cat purring. The five teens lowered their bodies to reduce wind drag and get maximum speed. The 'eggy Su' slipped through the waves like silk over glass and soon reduced the distance between the two boats. The roar of the engines and the regular rhythm of the hull crashing through the waves grew steadily louder. They could clearly see Renzo now, slumped over in the back seat, a red smear on the side of his head. There was no sign of Regina.

The teens kept up the pace and were able to catch up fairly quickly, but they were heading into the deeper water further from shore and away from the shelter of the island. The water would get deeper still as they headed further out to sea. The waves would be higher, the wind stronger, and the larger and heavier White Shark would manage better than the lightweight 'eggy Su'.

"What's the plan?" Ryan said.

"Get alongside, see what we can do when we've looked what's happening in there."

"If you can get close enough, I could jump over and take control," Terry said.

"No, it's too dangerous," Dawn insisted.

"What else can we do?" Terry asked. "We can't get in front of it and stop it that way."

"We could foul the props with something, that would stop it." Ryan suggested.

"We don't have anything that would work, unless we find a fishing net out here," Terry said.

"Which is possible, but it doesn't sound very controllable," Jenna said. "And the engines could catch fire if we can't shut them down fast enough."

"Let's try nudging it around into calmer water, then see what we can do," Conner said. "We're getting further away from help and the sea is getting rough."

The others agreed, and they were soon almost beside the White Shark. They could see Renzo Kneasley, who was still bleeding and appeared to have passed out. Regina was barely visible as Renzo had collapsed on top of her. Between that and her bound hands, it didn't look like she would be much help. The steering wheel had been tethered in place by a series of zip ties, so they couldn't lean into the boat and turn it. The twin throttles were low down in the center, so even further out of reach.

Conner mover closer, shrinking the gap, the 'eggy Su' bouncing higher and higher as the swell increased. The two hulls were almost touching now. He was very aware they were getting further from shore; he had to be careful but fast. With practiced use of the throttle, Conner carried on until he was able to nudge the 'eggy Su' against the bow of the White Shark. There was a squeaking and scraping sound as the two hulls touched. Conner increased the pressure slowly but the larger vessel wouldn't turn. Increasing their speed only sent the 'eggy Su' scraping along the speedboat's hull. They needed a more direct approach. Conner reduced speed and moved them away a little, then turned the 'eggy Su' so the bow was pointed at the White Shark, and took them back in. The bow bumped against the speedboat with more force than Conner had intended, but the speedboat responded, changing its heading a little. He twisted the throttle all the way open to keep the pressure on and the White Shark began to turn. He moved with it as it turned, keeping up the force against the hull. Both hulls were slippery with water and Conner lost contact, causing the 'eggy Su' to turn side on to the speedboat with a bump and a splash of cold water. He was forced to turn a wide circle and try again, the waves crashing against the side of the 'eggy Su' and splashing cold sea water over everyone for a second time.

Soon back in position, Conner moved in again and bumped the speedboat's hull, then pushed against it. The 'eggy Su' slipped again and was almost rammed by the White Shark. The maneuver turned the boat a little more but again Conner was forced to pull away. Glancing down, he saw they'd already used half the battery capacity and it was still dropping fast. With no other choice, Conner repeated the tactic, nudging the boat around and managing to hold position for a while longer. The two boats were now at different angles to the waves and he had to break off again, a fresh shower of sea spray washing over them every time he turned.

One more nudge and the speedboat was now heading south, which was better but not ideal. At least now he was cutting through the waves and not across them. He made contact bow first and tried again, attempting to move forwards and sideways at the same time. Conner discovered the secret was to give the speedboat a series of taps instead of one long push. With fine adjustments to the throttle and steering, he bumped and nudged the White Shark several times until it was facing back to shore and towards an area of calmer water. Now, of course, they had a different problem. They were heading straight towards land at maximum speed. Conner allowed the 'eggy Su' to return to her normal behaviour of moving in a straight line and moved into position next to the speedboat.

"I'll keep us alongside, try to grab it," Conner said as they entered a more sheltered spot and the high swell eased. They were on the port side of the boat, so Ryan and Jenna were able to grab the chrome rail around the White Shark's gunwale. Conner slowed, but the twin outboards were too powerful and the pair were forced to let go before they were pulled out of their seats.

"Conner," Terry said. "We seem to be heading back to Three Hills."

"What! We can't . . . oh. I turned us too far." Conner gasped when he looked ahead. "We might have to go around the other side and nudge them back."

"Too late now. Come on, try again, I'm going to climb aboard!" Jenna shouted.

"It's too risky!" Conner insisted.

"I don't think there's anything else we can do. They aren't running out of fuel but we're both running out of sea. Those engines are too powerful for us to stop any other way. Someone has to get aboard and turn them off." Jenna was already holding the rail.

"Ok, but wait one second. Terry, you still got that rope?" Conner said. "We can at least steady the two boats to make it a bit safer."

Terry reached into a pocket and pulled out the short rope they'd used to get off the spa roof. He quickly handed it to Jenna. She took the rope and passed one end of it through the rail on the White Shark and then passed both ends to Ryan; there was no time for a knot. With Ryan gripping the rope tightly, and Conner holding the 'eggy Su' steady, both hulls were in firm contact with each other. Barely waiting for the two boats to stabilize, Jenna pulled herself up until her stomach was over the gunwale, then she reached again to pull herself into the boat by the steering wheel. As soon as she was able, and with her feet in the air, she grabbed the twin throttle and eased it back until the speedboat slowed, pushed it into reverse for a few seconds and finally brought the powerful boat to a halt. Conner matched her speed and soon both boats were bobbing on the low swell a few hundred yards from the shallows around Three Hills Island. Jenna scrambled upright and into the helm seat, then turned off the ignition. The roar of the outboards ceased, and peace and quiet returned to the area. Ryan passed the rope to Conner and climbed into the back seat next to Renzo.

Once they were steady enough, Ryan and Jenna attended to the Kneasleys while Terry and Dawn kept a look out and Conner held them in place. Regina was in shock; she was very pale and her breathing was rapid. Renzo was still unconscious and had bled all over Regina and the back seat. The teens knew you weren't supposed to touch open wounds without gloves, so Ryan grabbed a clean part of Renzo's shirt and pulled him slowly upright; he didn't make a sound. They wouldn't normally have moved a casualty, but Regina was trapped underneath him and was obviously suffering. Jenna knelt on the seat and leaned over it towards the traumatized woman, then spoke to her calmly to get her attention and to slow her breathing.

"Just sit still for a few minutes, deep breaths in and slowly out."

Regina gave Jenna a puzzled look as she helped her up into a sitting position. "Do I know you?" she asked in a shaky voice.

"Just relax," Jenna said, trying not to let her expression give her away. "You're safe now. The Coast Guard should be here soon."

Using Conner's knife, Ryan cut Renzo's hands free then did the same for Regina. Although Regina looked at her husband a few times, she made no effort to care for him, just sat rubbing her wrists and taking deep breaths, occasionally glancing at the teens. They made the two as comfortable as they could and prepared to move off if no one came to help; now the outboards were silenced, the 'eggy Su' could easily tow the larger boat back to the harbor.

The first to arrive on the scene were a couple of pleasure boats. A Coast Guard helicopter followed shortly behind, clattering towards them from along the coast. Shortly after, the helicopter guided in a lifeboat and the Kneasleys were soon being cared for by professionals. While this was happening, Ryan and Jenna sneaked back into the 'eggy Su' and Conner pulled silently away from the White Shark. Then, mingling with the gathering crowd of boats, they slipped away and headed back to the harbor. Once they were away from the other people and couldn't be overheard, they began to talk about the situation.

"What do we do now?" Conner asked.

"We send the report like we usually do. Everything we have," Dawn said.

"And quickly, while the Kneasleys are in custody," Ryan added.

"I don't think they've been arrested," Jenna said.

"Maybe not, but they have a lot of explaining to do, like why they were tied up in a boat."

"Do you think they'll be honest?" Terry asked, "Or deny everything and try to wriggle out of it all like they usually do?"

"It depends on how scared they are of the Russians," Conner said.

"Very, I would say, especially after today."

"Ok, Dawn," Conner said, "Are you ready to send the evidence to the police?"

"Of course."

"Do you think we got them this time, the Kneasleys?" Terry asked.

Dawn nodded. "I would say so. There's some pretty serious stuff here and they're right in the middle of it."

Ryan looked around, grinning. "Is that it? Is this year's adventure over?"

Conner nodded, "looks like it."

"Hmm, ok. Wasn't bad."

The others laughed and then the conversation turned to other things.

From then on, the teens paid close attention to the local news sources. There was a brief report about a couple needing to be rescued when they lost control of their boat, and then nothing. The weeks flew by and summer headed towards fall. The teens continued their studies at the Maritime Academy, had more sailing lessons, camped out on various beaches, went on separate dates, and spent a lot of time playing video games.

On the last few days of summer, Dawn and Ryan found out from their dad and step-mom that Three Hills Island was up for sale. They then saw an article in the local paper about a business man and his wife having to sell their private island to pay legal bills. The situation rapidly snowballed and the next day it was all over every local news channel. The police had cracked a major drug smuggling operation, they claimed, and arrested dozens of people, include some foreign nationals. Drugs worth millions of dollars were found and destroyed. The main suspects, named as Renzo and Regina Kneasley, had all their assets seized and their bank accounts frozen and were now awaiting trial. In a press release, the police said only that they were acting on information they'd received anonymously. Which was exactly how the teens wanted it.

EPILOGUE

On the last day of summer, the teens cancelled all their dates and other commitments and headed off to Bear Cub Island, just the five of them. They camped in their usual spot, a piece of flat grassland above the beach. The nights were drawing in now and stars came out as the sky darkened.

"It's ironic, really," Conner said quietly.

"It often is, Con," Ryan replied.

"That we saved the Kneasley's lives so they could go to jail?" Dawn asked.

"Of course, we don't know for sure we saved their lives," Jenna said.

"No," Terry agreed, "they might have got their hands free, or ran out of fuel and rowed home, or bumped into a container ship and been picked up by it."

"Ok, we probably saved their lives," Conner insisted. "And we'll probably get as much thanks as we did from Marty Whitman."

"By the way, Ryan," Dawn said, "they did have pizza in 1812, or at least something like it. As far back as the Romans, people were eating flat bread with stuff on top."

Ryan smiled, "Cool. But still no internet."

Dawn laughed. "No, no internet. No games consoles, no smart phones."

"I feel sorry for them."

"No global warming, no seas full of plastic, no choking pollution," Conner said quietly.

"No antibiotics, no minimum wage, no health and safety," Ryan countered.

"No weapons of mass destruction, no genetically modified food, no instant noodles."

"Hey! What's wrong with instant noodles?" Ryan laughed. "It's what I'm living on when I go to college."

"Good luck with that, Ry."

They all fell silent and listened to the universe, each thinking their own thoughts. The waves lapped against the sand, a slight breeze hissed through the leaves on the nearby bushes, and small creatures rustled in the undergrowth.

Ryan sat up suddenly. "I've just realized something. If the Kneasleys are in jail next year, there'll be no one to commit crimes and no adventure."

Dawn laughed. "They aren't the only criminals in town."

"I know, but they were the most interesting, if you know what I mean?"

Conner nodded, "yeah."

"You know," Dawn said, "next year might be our last chance for adventure. We'll all be off to college after that, we might be scattered all over the country."

"Then we'd better make next year a good one," Ryan said.

Jenna laughed, "I don't think we have any control over that."

"Well," Dawn said brightly, "we could choose to just have a normal summer like everyone else. Or at least everyone else who has access to a fast boat, a yacht and the wide-open sea."

Ryan slumped back down onto his sleeping bag. "Boring!"

"Don't worry, Ry," Conner said. "I've got a feeling next year's adventure is going to be bigger than ever."

ABOUT THE AUTHORS

Author **Steve Wedlock** has lived a literal personal life afloat on the sea, with more than 350,000 nautical miles as master of many types of vessels, a Marine surveyor, a builder of schooners, a teacher of seamanship, navigation, and boat handling, and sea captain. Born and raised on the coast of Maine, this life became a part of him early on as a child—running around on the shore and rocks, fishing off lobster floats, and getting involved in boating as a youth. Steve's vast background in oceanic living brought him to want to share his knowledge and love of the sea and sparked his inspiration to share his stories. In the early 1970s, Steve wrote a private collection of seamanship subjects—weather lore, navigation, ship handling, systems—for his crew. Steve believes that interesting settings and realistic and relatable characters are what make a great children's story. A plot that has intrigue and protagonists that have conflict keep young readers engaged. *The League of Maritime Adventurers: The Ungrateful Rescue* is his debut middle-grade/young adult book in this series. He hopes that his book's young readers gain interest in the shores and oceans and that it encourages them to explore on their own with their friends. When Steve isn't writing thrilling mystery adventure stories for children, he enjoys a hobby in photography, using vintage cameras. He is currently retired and based in Antequera, Spain, spending three months a year visiting family in the United States, and another three months exploring new places in the world.

Steve Dean was born and still lives in the city of Nottingham in the UK. He began to read at a very early age and soon became an avid consumer of genre fiction. Over the years, he tried several jobs before ending up in IT support. During this time, Steve began writing his own fiction, eventually becoming a full-time freelancer. When not dreaming up strange monsters and robots, Steve plays tabletop and video role-playing games far too much, watches science fiction and science fact, and reads from his ever-growing library of genre novels. Just for a change, he also grows cacti and house plants, makes furniture, and tinkers with technology.

www.ingramcontent.com/pod-product-compliance
Lightning Source LLC
LaVergne TN
LVHW091326150826
845673LV00006B/1789

* 9 7 8 1 7 3 7 9 8 5 4 3 3 *